FATED

Book Two of the Bloodstone Saga

By

Courtney Cole

DEDICATION

"My mother had a great deal of trouble with me, but I think she
enjoyed it."
--Mark Twain

Mom, I'm pretty sure you didn't enjoy it, but I do hope it was
worth it.
This book is for you.

FATED

CONTENTS

Chapter One

Colored lights pulsed erratically in the dark gymnasium, creating odd reflections on the squirming mass of people on the dance floor. I squinted into the heat of the spotlight and gripped the microphone tightly as I scanned the room for the most important face. And I found him, as beautiful as anything I'd ever seen, laughing at a joke that I couldn't hear as he leaned against the doorway.

His bright, white smile was a beacon from across the room and I found myself wanting to drop the mic and run off the stage, straight to him. I imagined the way his arms would fold around me, holding me tightly to his chest and I fought the urge to act on my impulse. My need for him was almost palpable because any time that wasn't spent in his arms was just... wasted. Our time was always so limited.

I exhaled slowly as I felt the bass beat in my chest and I concentrated on the pounding rhythm to keep myself in the moment. I wasn't nervous and I wasn't afraid. My life was what it was. And I was okay with that. My issue now was a petty one. I was just second guessing our band's decision to play for Homecoming tonight. I would rather be dancing with Gavin right now rather than entertaining the student body.

My best friend Jessa picked up the tempo on her electric guitar and I felt my cue coming up. The air practically crackled with the music and I lifted the mic. Singing into it, I felt Gavin's eyes shift to me and I held his dark stare. His eyes were so dark that they were almost black. Endless, bottomless, total sexiness.

"Every breath is a promise and I swear, baby, I won't break it. You were meant for me, meant for me..."

I gyrated around the stage, ignoring the annoying way my leather pants clung to me, as I danced in time to Jenn on the drums. She was wearing thick black eyeliner and bright red lipstick tonight, the total opposite of the fresh-faced look that she normally shared with her sister.

My best friends, the Gray sisters, were identical twins, hence the name of our band, Macy and the Grays. Yes, we had secondhand equipment and yes, we practiced in my garage. But we loved it. We loved performing, we loved the attention, we loved actually writing the songs. We pretty much loved everything about it. And since we've been performing together since junior high, we've actually gotten pretty good at it.

Jess finished off her guitar solo, ending the song which wrapped up the set. I lifted the mic again, breathing hard.

"Thanks, guys. Hope you're enjoying Fall Homecoming! We're going to take a ten minute break. Don't go anywhere!"

I hopped down from the stage and found myself face to face with Gavin. His dark hair had gotten longer over the summer and it was now carelessly falling over one eye. He shook it out of the way and stepped closer to me.

"So, do you come here often?" he asked, grinning.

I sucked in my breath. His smile was breathtakingly beautiful. Especially when it was directed at me.

"Hmm, sometimes. Every day, actually."

"So, you would know a good restaurant..." he smiled and stepped even closer. I grinned back. He was copying our first meeting in the tiny deli in my neighborhood a few months ago. Corny, but charming at the same time. Of course, with that smile anything he said was charming.

"You haven't gotten any better at pick-up lines, just so you know."

I grabbed his arm and pulled him to me, burying my face in his neck. Closing my eyes, I inhaled the musky, cedar smell that belonged so specifically to him. And as we lingered in our intimate embrace, I knew that if I could freeze time right this second, I would.

To an outsider, we appeared just like any other teenage couple. We went to movies and got pizza and hung out and flirted. And technically, we had only met a few months ago. But I knew a secret. We've actually known each other for thousands of years. The problem is, *he* doesn't know that. *No one* else knows that.

I know it because I'm different.

I have a tiny birthmark on my wrist that marks me as a Keeper of Fate in an ancient organization called the Order of the Moirae. Life after life, my soul stays the same and I have the same purpose. I guide my Daedal through each life, ensuring that she makes the right decisions. And while keeping track of one person might sound easy, it is definitely not.

Because a Daedal always plays a vital role in history, which means that his or her life is never easy and it almost always ends tragically. Keeping mine on a collision course with destiny is not an easy task. But it is a necessary one. In a prior life, my Daedal was Cleopatra and I was her handmaiden, Charmian. Our deaths in that life were legendary. Cleopatra, my Daedal, hasn't found me in this life yet, so I had absolutely no idea what this life would bring. But I had no doubt that it would be interesting.

"Macy?"

I startled back to reality as Gavin searched my face quizzically.

"I'm sorry, I was spacing off. What did you say?" I focused on his handsome face, not exactly a difficult feat.

He smiled again and I consciously stilled my heart.

"I asked who you wrote that last song about. It wouldn't be me, would it?"

Cockiness radiated from his every pore but I loved that about him. I would be hard pressed, actually, to think of something I didn't love about him. He had a great sense of humor, was as loyal as the day was long and was as beautiful as an underwear model. I had lucked out in the soul mate department.

I leaned up to kiss him, but was knocked out of the way as Jess rushed up to us and grabbed my arm.

"You haven't even gone to the bathroom yet, Mace? You've only got a couple more minutes." She stared at me disapprovingly and then tugged at me. "Come on, say goodbye to Prince Charming and let's go get you taken care of. You are in desperate need of fresh lipstick."

I stared helplessly at Gavin as she pulled me away. He laughed and waved and I rolled my eyes.

As Jess dragged me toward the restrooms through the throng of people still milling about on the dance floor, I noticed my ex-boyfriend, Derek, standing on the periphery of the gym with his new girlfriend, Tara. The girl that he cheated on me with last year. The acrid taste of bile rose in my throat. Even though I knew that I was never meant to be with him, the mere memory of his betrayal turned my stomach.

Now though, I watched with interest as Tara shouted at him and he cringed away from her. Hmm. Apparently there was trouble in paradise. Someone should have mentioned to him that Karma was a venomous witch. What goes around comes around and maybe, just maybe, he was getting his. Was it wrong to feel happy about that?

I yanked on Jessa's arm.

"Did you see that?"

She nodded while she smirked. "I heard about it already. Apparently, he cheated on Tara. And they're trying to 'work through it'."

I should be embarrassed by the deep sense of satisfaction that I instantly felt, but I really wasn't. At one time, Derek's betrayal had cut me to the core. And now he had done it again to someone else. I guess it really was true- once a cheater, always a cheater. I would never have to worry about that with Gavin. I knew that with every ounce of my being. He was as steady as a beating drum. He always had been.

I glanced over my shoulder and found him staring at me, his dark eyes scorching me from across the room. He smiled a small, intimate smile and I felt warm all over. Nope. I would never have to worry about him in that way. Just one more perk of being a soul mate. I wrenched my eyes from him just in time to step into the girl's bathroom.

The brightness of the fluorescent lights seemed garish in contrast to the darkened gym and I blinked my eyes against it, staring at the dirty, pink tiled floor. Before I could focus, someone bumped into me and a sudden jolt of electricity almost dropped me to my knees. *No.*

Broken images flitted through my mind, like a deck of cards thrown into the wind... a pair of dark, twinkling eyes, glittering gold tableware, the sparkling Mediterranean Sea. *No. Not now.*

I could feel the Keeper side of me emerging, an unconscious awakening from deep within, guiding me to turn around, compelling me with a force that I couldn't resist. I had no choice but to stop in my tracks and pivot with the magnetic pull.

A girl was standing next to me, waiting her turn at the hand dryers. Small and slight, her chestnut colored hair was stick straight and hung to her shoulder blades. She glanced my way and I froze, my breath catching in my throat. I had seen her dark eyes a million times before. The last time I remembered staring into them, I had been saying good bye to her two thousand years ago, when she was Cleopatra and I was Charmian.

She was my Daedal.

My heart sped up, racing erratically against my rib cage. It was funny, I had known that I would come across her at some point, but being face to face with her now was alarming and emotional. It meant that my cycle was beginning again. Right now. This very second. From this point on, she and I would rocket toward our destiny. And I knew that it wouldn't end well. It never did, which meant my time was limited. I could practically feel hourglass sand dripping onto me. I gulped.

"Can I help you?" she asked, her dark eyes twinkling. At the sound of her voice, I jumped. I had been blatantly staring and didn't even realize it.

"I'm sorry, I didn't mean to stare. I was thinking about other things." For the second time in ten minutes, but I didn't point that out.

"Otherwise called, spacing off," Jess piped up. "Don't hold it against her. She does that a lot. She can't seem to help it."

Jess laughed and so did... Cleopatra. I briefly wondered what her name was in this life before deciding to just find out. I held out my hand.

"I'm Macy Lockhart. Are you new here?"

She grasped my hand and shook it, her hand small and delicate. A pinkie ring cut into my palm. I glanced at it and froze. It was amethyst. As Cleopatra, she had worn a massive amethyst ring on her middle finger. It was astounding how some things were always so similar.

"I'm Jade Greene. And yes, I realize the irony of my name. My parents must have strange senses of humor."

She rolled her eyes and smiled an impish grin. I sucked in my breath. She's always had that mischievous grin. It had gotten us both in and out of trouble more times than I could count. Also, the way she phrased that sentence gave me pause as though she was only guessing because she didn't know her parents. But I didn't ask.

Instead, I simply murmured, "It's nice to meet you."

She stared at me appraisingly, jutting her slim hips out.

"So, you must be the Macy from Macy and the Grays. I've gotta say-- you guys are awesome. I wish I had that much talent," she smiled ruefully.

"Oh, everyone is good at something," I replied. Such as being a legendary queen of Egypt. Jade was no slouch herself. She just didn't know it yet.

I turned to look at myself in the mirror. Dancing around on stage under the hot spotlights in tight leather pants had not done wonders for my makeup. My eyeliner was smeared and my hair was in wild disarray. Jade watched me examine myself and offered her makeup bag with a smile.

"Do you need this?" she grinned again, holding it out to me.

I sighed and grabbed it. "You're a lifesaver."

"Oohhh- can I borrow too?" Jess asked as she emerged from a bathroom stall. "My lips are dying for some gloss. And someone who will remain nameless left our makeup bags at her house. Macy."

I rolled my eyes as I ran a brush through my long dark hair. I couldn't help it. She had been rushing me, like usual.

"You've got gorgeous hair," Jade remarked. "But your eyes. Wow. They're amazing. I've never seen eyes that color of green. Are they real or contacts?"

I smiled because I get that a lot. My eyes are a startling, vivid green- so bright that they do seem like they should be contacts. In fact, they almost seem to glow. But I've had the same eyes in every life; it is one physical trait that has been constant. That and my dark hair.

I nodded. "They're real."

Jess elbowed me. "We've gotta go—Jenn's going to kill us if we leave her up there by herself."

I handed Jade back her make-up bag.

"Thanks again. And if you get bored and want to hang out sometime, give me a call. Do you have a pen in your purse? I'll give you my number."

She nodded and dug one out, handing it to me with an empty gum wrapper. I scrawled my number on it and handed it back.

"It was nice to meet you. Welcome to San Marino."

"Thanks. I'll call you soon- it would be nice to hang out."

I nodded and let Jess pull me out, wondering if Jade felt the same vague familiarity that I did. I was in the loop this time, though, and that was nice.

This cycle was different than any of my others, because my memories had already been unlocked. Normally, I live just like a normal girl until it is time for my cycle to begin, at which time, my Aegis (my handler, of sorts) appears to me and gives me my bloodstone, a powerful stone created just for me. The second I touch it, my memories are unlocked and my cycle begins.

But this time something unusual had happened. Because a mysterious high priest had tried to coerce me into undoing the past, my memories had been unlocked before my cycle even began. My Aegis, Ahmose, and I had to travel back to ancient Egypt in order to, well, save the world.

It had been gut-wrenching. Being back in Alexandria had been amazing. It had been as though I had never left, which was a little odd. But Gavin was there, in the form of Hasani, the commander of Marc Antony's armies. He was as beautiful as ever, strong and brave with a warrior's heart.

In every life, he was with me in some form. But in Alexandria, I had known he was going to die and how, which made every single second that we spent together wretchedly painful. I had ultimately managed to allow Fate to unfold as it was meant to, which meant that I had allowed a Roman soldier to run his sword through my soul mate. Hands down, it was the most difficult thing. Ever. In the history of the world.

And here we go again. My Daedal had found her way into my life. Which meant it was time for us to walk her difficult path yet again. I never had any real blueprint for the choices that she was supposed to make, but I had strong innate urges that guided me toward the right decisions. Plus, of course, the bird-shaped birthmark on my wrist throbbed like crazy when we were doing something wrong, sort of like a bad-decision compass.

As we wound our way through the crowded gym back toward the stage, I shook my head to get rid of my dark thoughts. There was no reason to stress about it now. One thing that I had learned after all of these years, was that no good came from worrying. What was meant to happen would happen. What I should do now instead of stressing, was spend every minute that I still had left with Gavin.

He was waiting for me at the base of the stage and I leaned into him, brushing a kiss against his soft lips. He smiled and I felt my knees literally weaken. He winked as I jumped up onto the stage, and I felt my heart crack just a little. He had no idea. He thought everything was fine. Normal. And normal it was not…the absolute story of my life.

Jenn started banging the drums and the throngs of people on the dance floor cheered, so I focused my attention on their faces, waiting for my cue to sing. The heat from the lights shone on my bare shoulders and I soaked it in now, while it still felt good. In about fifteen minutes, it would start getting too hot.

Allowing myself to become immersed in the moment, I concentrated on the bass thumping in my chest, tapping my foot to its beat. I could feel Derek's stare, Tara's glare and Gavin's soft gaze. And something else. Scanning the crowd, I searched for whatever it was that was making me feel...wrong.

Teachers lined the walls, dutifully supervising the hyped-up student body. Bodies writhed and undulated on the dance floor, stirring the subtle smell of sweat and the heavy scent of perfume. The colored lights flashed and shadows were cast against the walls. There was nothing out of place, nothing out of the ordinary. Everything seemed fine, but it wasn't. I could feel it.

Jess worked her way next to me and nudged me with her eyebrows raised and I realized that I had missed my cue. She back-tracked and played it again and I lifted the mic, singing into it absently as I continued to examine the room.

Jade stood alone at the back of the gym, moving gently in time with the music. It was painfully obvious that she didn't know anyone yet, since she was all alone surrounded by a crowd. I hoped she called me soon. She was bound to be lonely without anyone to talk to. She had always been a social butterfly.

Just as I was about to shift my attention, something about the way her eyes were fixated on the curtains lining the wall gave me pause. I peered more closely into the darkness, trying to see what she was staring at through the flashing lights. There was nothing there but suddenly, as she gazed at them, the curtains began fluttering--starting where she was standing and moving down the long wall like a subtle tidal wave. It took me a second to comprehend. She had done that.

I gasped but before I could react, a piercing pain ripped through me, radiating from my wrist. My birthmark throbbed wildly, spreading pain into my arm and quickly traveling throughout the rest of my body. The pain was so intense that I couldn't breathe. I dropped to my hands and knees, the mic flying from my hand and skittering across the stage. I vaguely recognized the shrill metallic feedback as it slid to a rest against a speaker. People covered their ears in the crowd as Jess ran to me and dropped to her knees beside me.

"Are you okay?" she asked frantically. "What's wrong?"

I struggled to breathe, trying to force air in past the pain. I couldn't speak. All I could do was shake my head and wrap my arms around myself as I laid on the floor, gasping for air. It was like a hundred knives were stabbing me, twisting and turning and wrenching.

"Macy, what is it? Do you need an ambulance?" Her eyes were flooded with panic as she was shoved out of the way by her sister. Jenn peered into my face worriedly.

"Macy, oh my God. Are you alright?" Jenn turned to the audience and screamed, "Someone call an ambulance!"

Gavin jumped onto the stage and sprinted to where I was lying. He dropped to the floor and picked up my hand as he loomed over me.

"Macy, look at me," he commanded. "Please, sweetheart, breathe. It's okay."

And I realized with a start that I still wasn't breathing. The pain wracking my body was preventing me from drawing a breath. I was still gasping like a fish out of water. And just when I thought it couldn't get worse, the pain spread to my temple, exploding into a million shards of light.

My last conscious thought was hearing my own scream.

Chapter Two

When I opened my eyes, the lights were blinding. Loud noises and hushed voices swirled around me and I squeezed my eyes closed again to shut out the dizziness.

"Macy?" A strange male voice asked. "Can you hear me? Squeeze my hand."

I squeezed his hand, but didn't open my eyes.

"She's responding to commands!" the stranger yelled. Suddenly, my right eye was wrenched open and a light shone into it. Then the left.

"Her pupils are equal and reactive to light!" he announced.

Something firm was strapped around my neck and I couldn't move my head. But I kept my eyes closed. My insides were on fire, a burning, gut-wrenching pain. If I just kept my eyes closed, I could focus on staying conscious. If I opened them, I might fade away. The pain was that intense.

And then I was moving. Someone was rolling me on a stretcher. It was a jolting ride. Every time they hit a bump, my insides screamed. Where was all this pain coming from? I'd never felt anything like it. Appendicitis, maybe?

All of a sudden, I dropped down as they unlocked the legs of the stretcher and then I was lifted back up manually. I opened my eyes.

The night sky yawned over my head, huge and black. Twinkling bright stars winked at me from the darkness and I stared silently at them, trying to focus on anything other than the blinding pain. I was still at the school in the parking lot.

And they were lifting me into an ambulance. I could hear Jenn's nervous voice and I summoned the strength to speak.

"Wait," I murmured. No one heard me in the melee. "Wait!" I croaked louder. Everyone paused and the man in charge looked at me.

"Where's Hasani?"

Everyone looked around in confusion and I realized my mistake. *Oh, god no.* My thoughts were so jumbled that I had called my boyfriend by a two-thousand year old name. I rushed to fix it.

"I meant Gavin. Where's Gavin?"

Gavin stepped into my line of sight and laid his hand on my arm. I focused on his face, which was calm in the midst of the swarming chaos around me. The familiar warm presence of his hand on my skin was calming.

"I'm right here, Macy," he answered quietly. "I wouldn't be anywhere else. I'm going to follow the ambulance and call your mom, okay? You're going to be alright. Do you understand?"

I wasn't sure if that was a directive or meant to be soothing but I nodded as best I could with the neck brace on. I felt his hand slip away from my arm and I wanted to protest, but I couldn't. He was gone and I couldn't see him anymore. They hoisted me into the ambulance and slammed the doors shut. A female EMT knelt beside me, cleaning my arm for an IV and talking to me in a soothing voice.

As I stared into her face, it morphed into the dark scary face of Annen, the high priest who had caused me so much trouble in Egypt. As the EMT murmured, all I could see were Annen's jagged teeth and I gasped, shrinking back into the stretcher. Just as soon as the sound came out of my mouth, though, her face returned to normal. Blonde hair, blue eyes, freckles on her nose. White teeth. Not the face of the high priest. She stared at me in concern.

"Are you alright?" she asked, with medical crispness. "Here, this will make you feel better."

She injected something into the IV and the walls of the ambulance got blurry as warmth spread quickly throughout my body. I closed my eyes.

* * *

I was suddenly standing in front of three women. And my pain was gone. The room we were in was cavernous and plain with white mist hugging the ceiling and swirling around our feet, clinging to my skin. I had no idea where I was and my disorientation only grew. There were no windows and I could see no doors, yet there was clearly a breeze blowing through, disturbing the strange white mist. It was curious. And I had no idea how I had gotten here. But no sooner did I even have the thought than I realized that I must be dreamwalking. This entire place was real, but it was appearing to me in a dream. It was disorienting.

The three women in front of me were sitting at a massive white marble table, each in an ornate carved chair. The woman sitting in the middle was glaring at me sternly, her thin lips pinched together tightly. Her skin was like parchment and I could easily see the blue veins in her hands and temple. Her pitch-black hair flowed to her waist, like an ebony river, pooling in her lap.

The woman to her right was small, very small. She had mousy brown hair, light brown eyes and a soft, heart-shaped face. She wasn't pretty, but she wasn't ugly, either. She was watching me sympathetically, her eyes liquid and soft, but something about her put me instantly on edge. Looking at her, I felt like I should feel comfortable, but she had the opposite effect. The hair on the back of my neck stood on end.

And I knew the woman on the left. White blonde hair, ice blue eyes, skin so pale it was almost transparent. She was scowling at me. It was Lachesis. The middle sister of the Fates and the one I had interacted with the most.

I was face to face with the three Moirae sisters. I gulped. This couldn't be good. Usually the Aegis stood in front of them and carried their wishes to the Keepers. I had never been summoned. Until now.

I took a step forward.

"Stay where you are," the woman in the middle commanded. "If I want you to come closer, I'll let you know."

She was clearly in charge which meant she must be Clothos. And that left the mousy little one to be Atropos. The one who controlled death itself. No wonder I felt uneasy. She was called The Unavoidable. And I suddenly realized what the mist was. It was my life force. Whenever any mortal was in the near vicinity of Atropos, their life force becomes visible. If she chose, she could inhale it which would kill me instantly. My foot faltered as I instantly stepped back and stood still.

A small smile lingered on her lips and I wondered briefly if she could read minds like Lachesis could.

"Yes, I can," she confirmed in a soft voice. Everything about her was so delicate and feminine, it was hard to believe that she could wield death with a mere whim. I cringed.

"Don't worry, little one," she assured me. "It isn't your time yet. I have no wish to harm you."

Clothos scowled.

"Speak for yourself, sister. I myself am quite agitated with her."

My head snapped up. What in the world had I done? I rattled through every possible thing that could have offended them, but came up empty.

"Now, now, sister," Lachesis said smoothly. "This situation isn't Macy's fault. That is your name in this life, is it not?" She stared at me coolly. She knew that it was. I nodded.

"You need to know that the Keres are gathering around you," Clothos explained, in the least gentle tone I'd ever heard. "Things are about to change, in a way so enormous, it is hard to comprehend." She sounded slightly excited about that last part, which seemed odd.

My confusion grew. I vaguely remembered Annen saying something about the Keres when I was in Alexandria. It was right after I had saved Hasani when he died saving my life. What had Annen said? *The Keres won't stand for this, Lachesis. I will try again and next time, I will not fail.* Afterward, I had asked Ahmose who the Keres were, and he had replied that it wasn't time for me to know.

I was guessing it was time now.

"And you would be correct," Lachesis nodded. I sincerely hated the whole mind-reading thing. Nothing was private from them.

"The Keres are our sisters. Our youngest sisters. They used to work with us, or rather, for us. They carried out the punishments of those who earned the worst deaths. But many years ago, they rebelled. They have been working against us ever since."

I stared at Lachesis, trying to make sense of what she had just said. If the Keres had carried out the worst punishments possible then they must be very scary people. At my thought, I saw Lachesis' lip curl slightly.

"Yes," she confirmed. "Our sisters shouldn't be taken lightly. They are fairly heartless."

Well, I suppose years of carrying out heinous executions would do that to someone. I tried to stop my imagination from running away with me, from trying to picture what they looked like and from wondering what these scary creatures wanted with me.

"So, the Keres have rebelled against you? What do they want?"

"Oh, who knows?" Clothos asked airily, waving her hand. "They wanted their independence and then they wanted to be seen as important in their own right and now… who knows? They are deluded. That much is certain."

She stared harshly at me.

"And they are inordinately interested in you, Keeper. Do you wonder why?"

I met her stare and tried not to flinch. Her eyes were as black as night.

"I don't know, Clothos. I didn't even know they existed until recently."

She cocked her head and examined me, probably rifling through my stored memories. Oddly, I felt nothing. Not even a tickle as she probed deep into my brain. After a few minutes, she nodded.

"Very well. I believe that you know nothing. But that doesn't mean that there is nothing to know. Your Daedal has always been of integral importance and it is truer now than ever. This time, she really does have the power to change everything. All will be revealed to you when the time is right. Until then, be on your guard, Keeper."

The Moirae suddenly started fading away, becoming more distant and more distant from me, until I could no longer see them. The mist swirled around me, clinging to my arms, legs and face and suddenly everything around me was consumed by the wispy whiteness.

And then there was nothing.

* * *

I was lying in a hospital bed, in a quiet dark room. After a startled gasp, I did a tentative once-over. I touched my arm—I was definitely here. This was real. And my pain was gone and this time it was for real. I was hooked up to an IV machine and I was wearing a hospital gown, but other than that, I seemed to be fine.

My mother was sleeping in a chair next to my bed. I briefly wondered where my father was, but then shook that thought from my mind. I already knew the answer. He was with his new girlfriend, of course. The 23-year old bleached blonde who used to be his receptionist. She was only six years older than me and had fake boobs that my father had probably paid for. It turned my stomach. I had told him that, too, a couple of weeks ago- a fact that probably explained his absence now.

I sighed. Oh well.

My mom stirred in her sleep and woke up with a start, her eyes instantly finding mine in the darkness. She sat up in a hurry.

"Macy! I didn't know you were awake. How are you feeling, honey?"

She brushed my hair back and her hand was cool. My life might be surrounded by supernatural craziness, but my mom was the same. Cool, comforting and always calm. She should've been an emergency room doctor instead of a dentist. She had nerves of steel.

I took a deep breath, trying to calm myself. It was confusing to be somewhere in my mind surrounded by supernatural beings and magic and then to return with no aplomb whatsoever to a perfectly normal hospital bed. It took a minute. I sucked in another breath. The air was so medicinal that I could taste it... iodine, peroxide, ointments, cleansers. Why did hospitals all smell the same?

"Macy?"

My mom was staring at me with her eyebrows raised.

"I'm sorry, mom. I'm just a little disoriented. What happened to me?"

She stroked my hand as she answered.

"We aren't really sure, sweetie. You were having unbearable pain and you were screaming and they sedated you. Your pulse was out of control... around 130 beats a minute. And then all of a sudden, you were still. And they haven't been able to find a source for your pain. Your blood work came back fine."

"How long have I been here?"

She looked at the clock and so did I. It was 3:30 am.

"About four hours. How do you feel now?"

I considered that. I wiggled my toes, bent my knees, flexed my fingers. I was fine.

"I'm okay. The pain is gone. That was so crazy."

"You're telling me. Don't do that to me again!" she wagged her finger at me and I rolled my eyes.

"Trust me; I would rather not have done it this time."

She smiled. "I sent Gavin home. He was right here by your side, but I knew his parents must be worried, so he left around an hour ago. Unwillingly, I might add. He'll be back first thing in the morning. Which will be any minute now." She was only slightly exaggerating. In a couple of hours, the sun would come up and I knew Gavin wouldn't be far behind.

"When can I go home?" I asked hopefully.

Mom shook her head. "I don't actually know. The doctor will come back in the morning. So, why don't we get a little more sleep and see what happens?"

I nodded in agreement and settled down in my bed, while Mom curled herself back up in the chair. My hand stung from the IV stuck in it, but I attempted to ignore it as I tried to force myself to go back to sleep. At the same time, I was a little scared to slip off into dreamland. I didn't like dreamwalking. When I woke up, I didn't feel rested and I always felt somewhat foggy. Not a pleasant feeling. Plus, facing the Moirae was terrifying.

After a few minutes of being wide awake and listening to the quiet footsteps of the nurses, I knew sleep wasn't going to come. There was just too much to think about. What had caused that horrible pain? Why were the Keres surrounding me? Where the heck was Annen in all this? The last time I had seen him had been in ancient Alexandria, when he had tried to convince me that the Moirae were just using mortals for entertainment. That there was no real purpose to fate.

I couldn't believe that was true. I just couldn't. If it was... then everything that I stood for was a lie. *I* was a lie. I purposely tried to avoid thinking about the other thing that Annen had told me.

I could be normal. I could renounce the Order and live just like a normal girl... never having to guide my Daedal into choosing decisions that would hurt her so much in the end. Because her decisions might help the world, but they certainly weren't all that good for her. Or for me. I sighed as I fingered the phoenix birthmark on my wrist.

My Daedal. The image of the curtains fluttering around her at the dance suddenly consumed me. She had moved them without touching them. How the heck had she done that? Clearly, something was drastically different this time. It was no time to bail on her. She would need me.

And besides, who knew what consequences such a drastic action would have? And what would happen to Jade if I quit? Although the idea of normalcy was so, so tempting. One of the strangest things about being a Keeper was that after my memories were restored, while I might not remember the details of past lives, I still kept the wisdom and experience that I gained from them... which made me a *very* unusual girl, a thousand (make that two) times older than my real age.

A nurse interrupted my musings, thankfully, as she came to take my vital signs. Apparently, my blood pressure was back down to normal, which she assured me was a very good thing. She poked and prodded at me for a few minutes, taking my temperature, chatting a little. I actually welcomed the company because I was afraid of my own traitorous thoughts.

As she bent back down to check my IV site, I glanced absently over her hunched back toward to door. It was standing open and I could see the nurse's station situated right down the hall. A nurse in yellow scrubs and a really bad haircut sat with her hands propped under her chin. It looked like she was trying desperately to stay awake. Every few seconds, her head slumped and she jerked it back up. I had to give her credit. Staying awake all night to work the night-shift night after night must be a nightmare.

As I absently stared at her, a black cloudlike fog appeared in my doorway and I startled. It quickly materialized into Annen. The priest's jagged, blackened teeth were stretched into a creepy grin as he calmly watched the nurse attend to me. I glanced frantically past him at the nurse in the hall to find that she hadn't moved. It didn't look like she had noticed anything. Couldn't anyone else see him?

He was the same as I remembered. His head was shaved, his eyes were black as night and his face was creased in wrinkles. Inky tattoos to the ancient god Anubis scrolled over his hands and up his frail arms, disappearing into the flowing dark robes. My heart pounded as the nurse finished messing with my IV tube and I prayed that she didn't notice my rapid pulse-rate. She straightened, smiled and walked out. Right through the bald priest. I gasped. She turned back around.

"Are you in pain?" she asked with concern, walking back to my bed.

I shook my head, keeping an eye on Annen in my periphery. He hovered motionlessly in the doorway, filling the entire doorjamb up with his presence. He blocked the light from the hallway. Couldn't she see that?

"There's no need to be brave, hon. The doctor ordered you pain meds, so you might as well take them." She punched some buttons on the IV machine and a few shrill beeps later, I felt a medicinal calm spreading through me.

"If you need anything else, buzz me," she instructed as she left. She didn't even flinch as she walked right through the priest's transparent body.

Annen floated toward me, stopping at the foot of the bed.

"Why are you here?" I hissed quietly. My mom stirred, but didn't waken. I was uncomfortable having Annen here, in the same room with her. I still didn't know what his real motives were or what exactly he was capable of.

He shook his head silently, his black cloak swirling around him even though he was standing still. He smiled one more creepy grin and then slowly pointed at my hand with one long, gnarled finger.

White hot pain instantly seared into my palm and I gasped, gripping my hand. After a long moment, the pain died and I released my hand, allowing my fingers to fall open. Words had been burned into my palm, as though someone had written them there with a flame-tipped pen.

Harmonia's Necklace

"Harmonia's necklace?" I whispered. "What is that?"

Annen just shook his head again. His silent routine was getting really old. He had never bothered to hold back his opinions before.

"What is wrong with you?" I demanded. "Cat got your tongue?"

He stared at me with his glittering black eyes for a moment before he opened his mouth wide.

Very wide. Where his tongue should have been, there was nothing now but a tiny stump. It had been cut out. I wanted to scream, but couldn't. A heavy, heavy weight formed in the pit of my stomach. I had a very bad feeling that his injury had been at the hands of the Moirae.

"Who did that to you?" I asked shakily. It had to have been someone very powerful. Annen had very, very strong magic of his own. He would have been able to protect himself against almost anyone. Except the Moirae. Or their sisters.

He shook his head again, as though my question was inconsequential and pointed once more toward my other hand. The white hot pain seared into me once again. I grimaced, but I was prepared for it this time.

"You know," I hissed. "A pen and paper would work just as well!"

I opened my hand.

Be careful.

"Of what?" I asked, looking back up at him.

But he was gone. I so hated their ability to do that. What was I supposed to be careful of? I opened my hands once again, just to re-read the messages, but like their author, they had disappeared. Not even a scar remained in their place.

I slumped back into my pillows. What did all of this mean? One of the most powerful priests that I knew had been mutilated by someone and was now trying to warn me. My own Aegis hadn't appeared to me yet and with everything going on, I felt vulnerable and helpless without my bloodstone. Not to mention that Jade was apparently more vital than ever to the Fates in this life. I had a terrifying feeling that my life this time around was really going to suck.

Chapter Three

"I still don't know what could possibly have been wrong with you," my mom fretted as she handed me a soda. The afternoon light poured into our kitchen, slanting across the sunshine colored walls. This room really was cheerful. It was probably my favorite room in the house for just that reason.

"Mom, you heard the doctor. I must have just had really horrible indigestion. Maybe I should stop having pizza for breakfast," I joked.

I knew it wasn't the two-day old cold pizza that had caused my intestinal agony, but what else could I say? That something supernatural had twisted my guts around until it felt like they were going to explode? Yeah. I could see how that would go over.

She shook her head. "I don't know. It just worries me."

I smiled at her. "And I appreciate it. But you can stop now because I'm fine."

She looked doubtfully over her shoulder at me as she loaded the dishwasher.

But I was thankfully saved by the doorbell. Our old dog, Hamlet, barely raised his head up from where he slept in front of the patio doors. I rolled my eyes his way.

"Don't bother getting up, Hammie. I'm sure it's no one dangerous."

I chuckled, but deep down, it was troublesome. Our old dog was getting older; his yellow muzzle had almost turned completely white. He rarely bothered to bark when the doorbell rang anymore, something that was entirely out of his character. I started to get up.

"Stay put, honey. I'll get it," mom instructed, turning to walk out. But I got up anyway.

"Seriously, mom, I'm not an invalid. I'm fine. It's Gavin, anyway."

I rushed to the front door- I just couldn't get there fast enough- and threw it open. Sure enough, my soul mate stood waiting for me on my porch. The sunlight bathed him in back-lit glory and I sucked in my breath, something I seemed to do a lot around him. As cliché as it sounded, he was always taking my breath away.

Today he was wearing a white button-up shirt with the sleeves rolled up and khaki shorts. The bright white offset his dark skin, making him all the more handsome. Beautiful, actually. And while it might be weird to call a guy beautiful, that was most certainly what he was.

"Hey," he greeted me, pulling me to him. He kissed me softly on the forehead and held me a moment. "Are you feeling better?"

I nodded, breathing him in. He was freshly showered and smelled like soap.

"Mmm-hmm."

"Are you lying?" he asked, as his chin rested on the top of my head.

"No. I really do feel fine. I think it must have been indigestion." How embarrassing to let my boyfriend think that I was laid-out by indigestion, but I didn't see what choice I had in the matter.

"Good. Then I have a great idea. Let's get you settled in on a lounger by your pool and we'll just hang out all day. You can rest."

"I don't need to rest!" I protested as he pulled me into the house. "I'm fine. Really."

"So sorry. Jenn and Jess are already coming over and they're bringing sandwiches. How else were you going to spend your Saturday, anyway? Hot plans with your other boyfriend?" He raised one dark eyebrow at me and I giggled.

"My *other* boyfriend realizes that I'm fine and that I don't need to be babied," I announced.

"Hmm. Your *other* boyfriend should watch out, then. I'm a jealous type," Gavin murmured, pulling me in close for another kiss on the forehead. "I'm glad you're okay. You scared me last night."

"I'm fine," I repeated. "Really."

"Yeah, that's what she keeps telling me, too." My mom breezed through the foyer. "I guess maybe she means it, but we should keep an eye on her anyway. Gavin, I've got some errands to run, so I'm counting on you for that."

"Definitely," Gavin agreed, as we followed my mom through the kitchen. "I'll take good care of her for you."

Mom nodded and grabbed her keys. "Macy, I seriously do want you to take it easy today. If you start feeling bad again, call me on my cell immediately."

"Yes, Dr. Lockhart," I teased. "Apparently, I'm going to spend the afternoon by the pool doing nothing, so you don't have anything to worry about."

She nodded in satisfaction. "I'm glad Gavin can keep you in line. Someone needs to."

"Whatever," I grumbled. "Between all of you, I've got enough babysitters to last a lifetime."

As soon as we stepped outdoors, though, my agitation faded. The sun was out, the sky was blue, the clouds were fluffy and white. It was a perfect California day. The blue water of our pool glistened as the breeze blew slight ripples across the top. How could I stay grumpy? The birds were even singing.

"Okay," I sighed as I settled into a pool lounge. "Maybe I can handle this today."

"That's what I thought," Gavin replied as he set down my cell phone and soda on the little table next to me. Stretching, he opened the umbrella over us and I sighed again. I had to admit. It was perfect.

Gavin reached over and held my hand and we laid there silently in the sun, just enjoying the warmth and each other's presence.

And then my cell phone rang, interrupting the silence.

"It's Jenn," I guessed as I reached for my phone. "Wanting to know if I want pickles on mine."

But it wasn't. I glanced at the screen and didn't recognize the number.

"Hello?"

"Hi... Macy? This is Jade Greene. We met last night and you gave me your number. I just wanted to call and make sure you were alright. For some reason, I didn't sleep very well last night. I tossed and turned, wondering if you were okay."

Of course she did. Keepers and their Daedals had inexplicable bonds. She didn't know that she was my Daedal, but she was already feeling the invisible tie that kept us close. The thought that she was feeling it too should be comforting, but for some reason, I really just felt a strong sense of unease. Something was different this time. And I wasn't sure that I liked it.

"Hi Jade. I'm glad you called. I'm feeling so much better. In fact, my boyfriend and I are just hanging out by the pool, soaking up some vitamin D. We have some friends coming over and they're bringing lunch. You're more than welcome to come over too, if you'd like, and get to know them. It should be fun."

I gave her my address and as we hung up, I heard Gavin already on the phone with Jenn, asking her to bring more food. When he hung up, he looked at me.

"Who is this Jade girl?" he asked curiously.

Oh, just someone I've known for two thousand years — you've protected her with your life over and over. Which is what I wanted to say. When Jade was Cleopatra, Gavin was Hasani, the leader of Marc Antony's armies. He laid his life on the line for her and in fact, that was how he had ultimately died. But obviously, he no longer remembered that little detail and I wasn't at liberty to refresh his memory.

"I met her last night in the bathroom," I answered. "She seems really cool and I think you'll like her."

"I like everyone," he pointed out, grabbing my hand again.

"True," I agreed. "But she's new and I thought she looked like she could use some friends."

"You're a softie," he replied. "So out of character for a goddess. But I love that about you."

"A goddess. I like that," I murmured, closing my eyes.

I loved the feeling of a good sun bath — the way the sun wrapped my body in warmth. I also enjoyed the way Gavin's hand stroked mine, even when we were practically asleep. We were so in tune with each other that I knew where his body was even when my eyes were closed. Just one perk of being a soul mate, I guess.

A dark cloud stepped in front of my sunshine, though and I scowled as I opened my eyes. Jess hovered over me with her hands on her hips.

"So, you know, Mace, if you wanted some R&R, you could have just said so. You didn't need to bail out on Homecoming in an ambulance to do it. Talk about dramatic exits!"

She grinned and tossed a rolled up sandwich on my lap.

"Do you need anything else? Another soda, a fresh pair of sunglasses, a pedicure? I don't want you to start feeling neglected."

I rolled my eyes at her sarcastic banter. Gavin sat up as he unwrapped his sandwich and turned to me.

"Do you feel neglected, Macy? Because say the word and I'll totally bring my A-game."

"Hmm. Like maybe handcuffing me to my bed or…?"

He raised an eyebrow suggestively at me and I punched him lightly on the shoulder.

"Because that's the only way you could keep an even closer eye on me. Get your mind of the gutter, mister!" I laughed as I turned my attention back to Jess.

"Seriously, you really don't need to babysit me, you guys. I'm fine."

"Save it, Macy," Jenn instructed as she settled on the teak lounger to my left. "We're here to annoy you all day. Don't ruin it for me."

"Don't kill your mellow?" I asked with a smile.

"Exactly. I'm glad you understand," she nodded, taking an enormous bite of her sandwich. "The sun is out, I'm going to lay by the pool *and* I get to eat carbs today. It's a banner day."

I rolled my eyes again. Both she and Jess were rail thin. Tiny little wisps of girls. There was no need to restrict their diet of anything, much less bread and pasta, my two favorite things in the world. But she was adamantly sticking to it. And so far, she was still the same exact size as her sister.

"Whatever," I replied, shaking my head. I glanced around the pool area. The rest of the lounges surrounding the pool were empty, as was the hot tub.

"Where's Jess?"

"She's in the house arranging your Sick Day tray."

"My what?" I looked at her suspiciously.

"A tray of stuff that any sickly invalid needs," she smirked.

"You're a brat. Just so you know."

"So I'm told," she nodded.

At just that moment, Jess opened the patio doors, stepping carefully down the steps with a huge tray. I could see magazines, a book, my iPod, a bag of cookies, a stack of sliced cheese and a loaf of Hawaiian bread (my all-time favorite) and several bottles of nail polish.

"Aww—you're too good to me," I said as she set the tray down on Gavin's lap.

"I know," she answered back confidently.

"You're a brat too, though," I added.

"Oh, I know that, too," she replied cheerfully. She stripped off her shirt and revealed a new bright red bikini.

"Wow! Look at you, little Miss Hottie! Love the swimsuit!"

"I know, right? And I haven't even given up carbs."

"Bite me," Jenn called from her position across the pool. "Seriously, don't mess with me. Perpetual lack of bread makes me bitchy."

"Don't we know," Jess muttered under her breath as she arranged her towel under her.

"What was that?" Jenn called.

"Nothing, dear sister. I said nothing at all."

Jess finally got herself all arranged and stared at me.

"So, what's up with this new chick?"

"I don't know. She seemed lonely, so I thought I'd invite her to join us. That doesn't bother you, does it?"

"Of course not. I know I'm your favorite."

"Not true," Jenn called, scowling at her sister. "I am."

Sensing a twin-sized argument coming on, I stepped in.

"You're both my favorites," I interrupted diplomatically. It apparently appeased them because Jenn settled back with a magazine. They were so competitive that it made me laugh.

Satisfied with her importance in my life, Jess leaned back in her chair and tilted her face to the sun.

"I could get used to this," she mumbled.

Hammie interrupted our serenity, though, with frantic barking and I sat straight up in my seat. I couldn't even remember the last time he'd barked like that.

I jumped up and ran into the house, with Gavin close behind me, ever protective. It was still weird to me how personality traits pass down throughout the millennia. He was a protector just like he'd always been.

The dog was jumping at the door, trying desperately to get through it. I grabbed his collar.

"Hammie, what in the world has gotten into you?"

I peeked through the peep hole to find Jade standing on the porch. She was holding a big bakery box and bouncing up and down on her ankles nervously. I wondered if she'd heard my dog going bat-shit crazy over the doorbell.

Gavin grabbed Hammie's collar from me as I opened the door.

"Hey Jade! So glad you could come. Please come in and ignore my dog. He's about a hundred years old in people years, so he won't hurt you. I don't know what's wrong with him."

Hammie was practically frothing at the mouth as he lunged against his collar to get to her and Jade stared at him doubtfully.

"Yeah, he looks like a sweetie."

In response, he bared his teeth and growled at her.

I tapped his nose lightly and dropped to my knees to get in his face.

"What is *wrong* with you?" I shook his collar and glanced up at Jade. "I think we'd better close him up in a spare bedroom so that he doesn't bother you. Do you have cats or something? Maybe he smells them."

Jade shook her head. "Nope, my house is a pet-free zone. My grandma is allergic."

Her grandma. I made a mental note of that. She lived with her grandma instead of her parents. Interesting.

"Well, I apologize. I don't know what has gotten into him."

She smiled graciously. "It doesn't matter. Here- I thought you could use some cupcakes. I hope you like death-by-chocolate."

She thrust the box at me and I glanced at the top. They were from a gourmet bakery downtown. She had gone to some trouble to get them.

"What girl doesn't?" I replied with a grin. "Thanks, although you didn't have to do that."

I handed the box to Gavin.

"Could you take these and Jade out to the pool, pretty-please? I'm going to contain this guard dog in a spare room."

He nodded and willingly led Jade out the back as I put a chew toy and Hammie in an empty bedroom. He was perfectly calm now, as though he hadn't a care in the world. He dropped onto his side and promptly closed his eyes, not interested in the slightest in the chew toy. His agitation was forgotten.

I shook my head as I closed the door behind me. Crazy dog.

As I emerged onto the deck, I found that everyone else had already descended upon the cupcake box.

"Hey! I'm the invalid! Save some for me!"

I shoved Jess over just in time for Gavin to put a bite in my mouth. I froze as the creamy chocolate frosting melted in my mouth.

"Oh my gosh. This is..." I was at a loss for words.

"Unbelievable? Incredible? Orgasmic?" Jess offered.

"Something like that." I took another bite. "Wow. These are amazing. Jade, you're my new hero."

She grinned as she licked her fingers. "I know. I try not to go this bakery very often or I'd end up on a carb-free diet, too."

She looked as Jenn, who so far was abstaining from the cupcakes, but her knuckles were turning white as she gripped the arms of her lounger.

"Why are you giving them up, anyway? You're so tiny!"

Jenn relaxed her hold on her chair and smiled at Jade.

"Thank you. I think you just became my new favorite."

I tuned out their friendly chattering and focused in on Gavin. He was staring at the pool with an absent expression. I would never get tired of studying his face. The cleft in his chin, the cut cheek-bones, the dimples when he smiled. I suddenly had a clear memory of him standing on the edge of the Alexandrian Bay with a sword in his hand and shaking the water out of his hair. He had always taken my breath away. I shook myself out of it.

"A penny for your thoughts?" I offered softly.

He looked at me. "Only a penny?"

"Nope. Name your price. If I have it, it's yours."

He grinned and I sucked my air in. I would never, in a million years, get used to his beautiful smile.

"Really?"

"Definitely. Name it," I confirmed.

"Alone time. Just for a minute. I want you all to myself."

"Done," I declared, immediately getting up from my seat.

"Gavin," I said loudly as I got up, "I think you left your swim trunks in the pool house last time you were here. I'm going to go check for you." I stared at him pointedly over my shoulder.

"I'll come with you," he offered, his smile turning devilish.

Ignoring the teasing from the girls, I pulled him into the little pool house and immediately pushed him gently against the wall directly inside the door.

With my face barely an inch in front of his, I whispered, "Okay. We're alone. Was there a particular reason you wanted me here?"

My lips brushed his as I spoke and I felt a current of electricity spark between us. Warmth instantly flooded into my nether-regions and I pushed myself up against him. The contact was delicious and I wanted more of it.

He might not have the same warrior's body that he had when he was Hasani, but he was still strong and sexy in a very modern way. He bent his head and lightly kissed my neck from my ear to my collar bone. Goosebumps formed everywhere his lips touched and I shivered.

"You scared me yesterday," he murmured, as he rubbed the goose bumps away.

I couldn't think straight with him touching me.

"You mentioned that. And I'm sorry," I mumbled as I pushed my hands up under his t-shirt and skimmed over his chest. His skin was warm and smooth under my fingers. I felt him react to my touch and smiled.

"You definitely did," he confirmed sternly. "Don't do it again."

"Or what?" I asked innocently, right before I nibbled at his earlobe. I felt him shiver.

"Or I'll have to get to get all Neanderthal on your ass. Maybe I really will chain you to your bed." He glanced down at me. "And don't look at me like that. You won't enjoy it."

"Hmmph." I stuck my nose in the air and pouted. "It's not like I meant to get carted off to the hospital in front of the entire student body. Everyone is just over-reacting."

"First, you don't have to stop doing what you were doing," he grinned wickedly at me. "And second, Macy, you have been under a lot of stress lately. With your parent's divorce and everything and the nastiness over your dad's girlfriend... you just need to take a step back and recharge."

He had no idea about the stress I had been under.

As I pondered that for a moment, I stared absently out the boathouse window, watching the girls walk into the house. Gavin ducked his head again and pressed his soft lips against mine and I closed my eyes. Who could think with those lips around? I lost myself in his kiss for a few minutes, all the while trying to will my knees to not give out. Pathetic, I know.

He ended the kiss and grinned cockily at me. "There's more where that came from, if you promise to behave yourself from now on. No more stress."

I nodded. "Yes, sir."

Out of my periphery, I saw Jade come back out of the house, struggling to juggle an armful of cold soda cans and open the door at the same time. The door stuck for a moment in its usual annoying way and then slid abruptly open. She wasn't expecting it and she fell headlong down the steps, the soda cans flying every which way.

She sat up, stunned for a moment, as blood ran down her arms from the huge scrapes on them. I gasped, twisting out of Gavin's embrace and running for her.

I bounded across the pool deck and dropped to her side with Gavin close behind me.

"Are you okay?" I demanded. "That stupid door. We keep meaning to get it fixed, but haven't gotten around to it. With my dad gone…" but Jade interrupted.

"I'm fine, really," she assured me. "Nothing to worry about. I'm just clumsy."

She wrapped her arms around her waist and stared uncomfortably at me.

"No, you're not," I insisted. "You're bleeding. I'm so sorry. I'll go get you some bandaids…" my voice trailed off as I noticed her arms and I stared at her in amazement. "Um, your arms…"

She stared back at me calmly. "What about them?"

"I was watching from the pool house. You were all scraped…" My mouth gaped open.

Because she wasn't now. Fat droplets of blood were splattered onto her shirt, but her arms were completely smooth and injury-free.

Chapter Four

$\mathcal{G}$avin and I stared at each other for a minute, before we turned to look at Jade again in perfect unison.

"It was nothing," she insisted. "Just a little scrape, but I wiped it off on my shirt. I'm fine."

She bent down to pick up the scattered soda cans.

"I'm sorry that I spilled everything. I'm clumsy. I shouldn't have tried to carry so much."

I felt my mouth drop open and I closed it. One thing my Daedal was not: Clumsy. She never had been. Gavin and I knelt to help her pick up the mess. Out of the corner of my eye, I examined her arms again. Absolutely not a scratch on them. Unbelievable.

"It's okay. Don't worry about it," I answered.

Gavin carried the soda cans to the nearest table and stacked them neatly in a small pyramid.

"Where are the girls?" he asked curiously.

"They went in search of some sun block. But your dog seriously doesn't like me. I think he could smell me through the door and he practically tried to break the door down to get to me. So I figured I'd replenish our supplies."

"That's so weird," Gavin mused. "That old dog likes everyone. Kind of like me," he added with a grin.

"You're a dog?" I asked. "You'd better not be. I expect you to be in tip-top gentleman form."

"Yes, m'am," he saluted, grinning so that his dimples showed.

"You guys are cute," Jade observed with a smile. "How long have you been together?"

Oh, a couple of millennia.

"A couple of months," Gavin answered. "But I feel like I've known her for an eternity."

Because you have.

I abandoned my snarky thoughts and turned my attention to Jade.

"So what about you? Do you have a boyfriend?"

"Nope. I had one, but we broke up right before I moved here. It was for the best."

Absolutely. Because you're meant for Marc Antony…or whatever his name is now.

Gavin turned to me. "You know who she'd be perfect for?"

I shook my head. "No. Who are you thinking of?"

"Noah."

I smiled. "You're right. Noah would be perfect."

Calm, loyal, handsome, half-back on the football team… Noah Chamberlin was an all-American boy who any girl would fall in love with. He was also boring. I knew Jade would lose interest in him eventually, probably sooner rather than later. But that was fine. She didn't need to fall in love with someone other than Antony. It would be complicate things. So Noah was a perfect temporary distraction.

"Okay, spill!" Jade demanded. "Who is Noah and when can I meet him? I'm just a poor, lonely new girl. I need some excitement."

I pulled out my phone and chose a picture of Gavin and Noah from the last football game and turned the screen her way. Noah's all-American boy charm made its way through the picture just fine.

"He'll do," she breathed and I laughed.

"Okay. How about… we all four go out for pizza tomorrow night? Group date!"

"Perfect," she agreed. "Should I come here or meet you somewhere?"

"Oh, just come here. We can all ride together."

"I'll drive," Gavin offered. "That way, you don't have to take your life in your hands in Macy's car." I swatted him on the arm as he laughed. I didn't know why everyone teased me about my driving. It was as good as anyone else's.

"I'm a great driver!" I insisted as he laughed.

"Prove it," Jade said laughingly. "Could you possibly drive me home? My car is in the shop and I had my grandma drop me off. I'm not feeling that great. I think I got too hot in the sun. I don't live that far from here."

"Of course I can. And we'll get there safe and sound," I assured her. "Don't even listen to Gavin."

"I'll be by the pool," Gavin said. "Safely lounging in the sun. May the force be with you, grasshopper," he added to Jade.

"You just butchered two separate movies," I pointed out. "But the joke's on you anyway. I'm a great driver. As you will see," I added for Jade's benefit. She nodded trustingly as we headed for the house.

I stopped in the doorway. "You know," I mused. "You should borrow a shirt from me to go home in so that you don't give your grandma a heart attack when she sees the blood on yours."

"You don't have to do that..." Jade started, but I interrupted.

"Oh, please. I have tons of clothes and it's the least I could do. It was my deck that you tripped on."

I led her to my room and sure enough, as we passed the spare bedroom, Hammie went crazy, jumping and scratching at the closed door. Weird dog.

We stepped inside my room and she looked around as I headed for the closet.

"Wow, you're so neat."

And I was. I always had been. I hated chaos, which was weird, considering how my lives always played out. Usually the only thing out of place in my bedroom were shoes. I had so many of them that I had run out of space in my closet. My one indulgence. Well, besides my car, but I had never asked for that.

I grabbed a shirt for her and stepped back out of my closet. As I tossed it to her, I noticed a slight glimmer from the corner of my eye and turned toward it. My bloodstone necklace was draped across my pillow. I tried not to show any surprise at all. I had known this was coming, obviously. Jade was already in my life. I had been expecting my Aegis, Ahmose, to appear at any moment with my bloodstone. But still. It was slightly startling to find it just sitting on my pillow.

Before Jade saw it and could reach for it, I strode across the room and picked it up.

Instantly, visions assailed me and I closed my eyes for a moment, immersing myself in what I saw. Jade was stretched out on a hospital bed with tubes and hoses running in and out of her. Her eyes were closed, her face was pale. No one else was there- the room was entirely sterile and devoid of any human element. She was surrounded by draped plastic and the buzz of machines. I dropped the bloodstone into my top dresser drawer and the vision stopped.

I exhaled slowly and turned around. Jade looked at me with concern.

"Are you feeling okay? You're really pale."

I smiled slightly. "Not everyone is blessed with your skin tone, Jade. I'm fine."

She kept talking but I tuned her out as I concentrated on stilling my rapid breathing before she noticed that, too. The vision had been alarming. Wherever Jade had been, it didn't look like a normal hospital. And then a detail that had been nagging my subconscious hit me square in the face.

Her hands had been restrained to the sides of the bed.

What the hell? This was the part of being a Keeper that I hated. Something bad always happened to her. And she didn't deserve it. It wasn't fair that she was condemned to live tragedy over and over. Granted, it was normally just a little different for me since I usually didn't have vivid memories of any past lives. My bloodstone revealed glimpses to me, but certainly no details. But still. She didn't deserve it.

The injustice of everything was starting to weigh on me heavily. I just couldn't help but wonder if anything at all that Annen had told me was true. Was there a plan? Or were we all simply puppets for the Fates to pull our strings?

I shook the thoughts from my head and smiled once again at Jade.

"Are you ready?"

She nodded. "I really appreciate you taking me home."

"Seriously, it's no trouble. I'm sorry that you're sick."

She shrugged. "It's no big deal- I just don't handle the sun well."

I had to stop myself from gaping at her bald-faced lie. She loved the sun and always had. I suspected her sudden departure had more to do with the fact that I had witnessed her miracle healing. And I would ponder that little episode later.

We walked through the house and into the garage and she stopped, staring at my little black car.

"A Lexus? I'm impressed."

"Don't be," I grimaced. "It's was just part of an elaborate strategy. My dad's plan to get under my mom's skin, that is.

And besides, I think it's the smallest Lexus on the face of the planet."

"Still," Jade replied. "It's nice. Way better than my deathbox. At least yours is new."

I backed out of the garage, coming dangerously close to clipping my side mirror on the garage door, a fact that I hoped she missed. She didn't say anything, so maybe it went unnoticed.

We were quiet for a while as I drove and the silence wasn't at all uncomfortable. I knew this girl inside and out and she knew me, too. She just didn't remember it. Minor detail. But I sensed that she was comfortable with me, too.

She hadn't been lying. She only lived ten minutes away in a quiet little neighborhood to the south of me. I turned into the driveway of a cozy little cottage with blue shutters. It was a tiny little house, but the yard was immaculate and full of blooming colorful flowers. An elderly woman knelt in a flowerbed, crouching over a bed of pink tulips- my favorite.

As I got out of the car, I called, "Your tulips are beautiful!"

She turned and offered me a crinkly grin.

"Thank you, dear. They are an enjoyment to me." She glanced at Jade. "Hi, sweetheart. I didn't know we were having company. Or I would have cleaned up." She sounded just the slightest bit disapproving and I wondered at it. But then she smiled again, so I dismissed my thought. I must have been mistaken.

"Grandma, this is Macy Lockhart. She volunteered to drop me off so that I didn't have to bother you with it."

I paused at her lie, but decided it wasn't a big deal. A giant Buick was parked in the driveway. She probably just hadn't wanted to ride around in a grandma car. I couldn't blame her.

"Well, I'm glad to you meet you, Macy," she smiled. "I'm Gladys, Jade's grandmother. I'm happy that she's met a new friend. California is a big place." She turned to Jade. "Jade, take this poor girl in. She shouldn't be standing around after her troubles yesterday. Are you feeling better?" she peered at me.

"I feel much better, Gladys. Thank you for asking. They think it was just a bad case of indigestion."

She peered at me again. "No doubt from all the junk you teenagers eat. You really should eat more fruit. It's good for you."

Jade scowled good-naturedly at her grandma. "Gran, you don't even know how she eats. Maybe she's a health nut. You don't know."

"Well, take her inside anyway. And get her some lemonade. It's fresh-squeezed," Gladys added.

Jade led me inside the tiny house and the inside was just as neat at the exterior. Crocheted doilies, flowered wallpaper, yellowed still-lifes on the walls. All of the quaint things you would expect from a grandmother's house. My grandparents had all died before I was born, so I didn't have any real experience with them.

Jade poured me a glass of lemonade and led the way to her room. I trailed behind her, taking everything in. There were pictures of her grandpa on the wall, but there was no sign of him at all in the house. He must have already passed away. It was just Jade and her grandma in this house.

She pushed open the door to her room and I gasped.

"Holy crap! It's like a whole other world in here!"

The entire room was full of state of the art technology...a huge flat screen was mounted on the wall, surround sound speakers were hanging from the corners, a brand new laptop adorned a sleek mahogany desk. Her furnishings were modern and plush and starkly out of context in the quaint little house. I turned to her in amazement.

She shrugged her shoulders. "My parents live in Switzerland and they want to be able to chat with me every night via webcam."

"Um, my crappy old laptop has a webcam. This is… this is…" I gestured toward everything in her room. There were no words.

"Yeah, I know," she muttered and she actually blushed. "It's serious overkill. But my dad is a scientist and he likes gadgets."

"Why do you live here, if your parents live in Switzerland?" I asked curiously. "Am I being too nosy?"

She smiled. "No, of course not. It's a valid question. My dad works for a biological engineering company and their corporate office is secluded in the mountains. My parents didn't want me isolated up there so they left me here to go to a normal, American school."

"Just now? When did they leave?"

"Oh, no. They've lived there for years. I was going to a private school, but my grandma just decided that a public school would be good for me. And so here I am… a brand-new student in my senior year at San Marino."

"Don't worry," I murmured comfortingly. "You'll be fine. You know me now … and Jenn, Jess and Gavin. And tomorrow you'll known Noah. Don't blame me though when he bores you to tears."

She grinned. "I think somehow I'll manage. You know, what with being blinded by that smile and all."

"He *is* pretty," I agreed. "I'll definitely give him that."

"So you'll call me about tomorrow?" Jade asked hopefully, as she showed me to the front door.

"Yep. I'll talk to you tomorrow." I walked toward my car. "Thank you for the lemonade," I called to Gladys. "It was delicious."

"You're welcome, dear. It was very nice to meet you. I'm glad my Jade has a new friend." She waved and went back to weeding her flower bed. I turned up the volume on my stereo as I backed out of the driveway.

As music dulled my senses, I thought about what I had just seen. It was very, very curious.

Why had her parents left her at her grandma's like that? Knowing my Daedal's propensity and not to mention biological inclination toward all things out of the ordinary, I knew there had to be a reason. And it was probably an essential key to our path in this life.

"And you would be correct." Ahmose appeared in my passenger seat, just as breezy as could be.

I startled, but maintained my grip on the steering wheel. He looked the same as he always did with his shaved head and thick, kohl-rimmed eyes. I briefly wondered why. Why did the Aegis persist in wearing ancient clothing- long robes and traditional make-up, when it was so obviously out-of-date? Apparently, fashion wasn't a priority for them.

"You know I hate it when you do that, priest," I gritted through my teeth. "One of these days, you'll give me a heart attack."

"What would you have me do? Make an appointment?" he asked innocently. I rolled my eyes.

"Thanks for bringing my bloodstone back," I acknowledged.

"You're welcome," he nodded.

"Now tell me... what's the deal with Jade? There's something different about her this time. And I had a vision that she was strapped to a hospital bed."

He nodded again, but ignored my question.

"Jade's father is a very important man in scientific circles, Macy. He's a molecular engineer. And he left Jade in her grandmother's care to keep her safe."

My eyes flew to his onyx ones. "Why? Is something threatening her?"

"Nothing yet. But once word gets out about what she is… the whole world will want her and there are those that would prevent that from happening."

Confusion clouded my thinking. "What do you mean? What is she?"

At just that moment, a deer bounded into the road and I screamed, yanking on the wheel—the exact opposite of what I should have done. My efforts were futile, anyway. With a sickening crunch, we plowed into the deer before the car careened into the ditch.

On impact, my air bags exploded, throwing my head against my seat with such force that I felt my nose snap. As the car settled to a stop, I sat stunned. I lifted trembling fingers to my face and they came back bloody. I glanced into my rearview mirror. Blood gushed from my broken nose and I gingerly wiped at it.

I looked out my window. The deer was a bloody motionless mess on the side of the road.

"Oh, crap," I whispered, putting my fingers to my head again.

Ahmose laid his bony hand on my arm. "Are you alright?"

He was perfectly calm, almost as if he had expected the deer's surprise entrance into our lives.

"Yes," I muttered. "I mean, I think so. Better than him, at any rate." I gestured toward the dead animal.

Ahmose turned my chin around with his fingers and then pointed at my bloody face. I literally felt the throbbing pain suck out of my body as the bones and cartilage of my nose realigned. He dropped his hand and I looked at my wound in the mirror. It was no longer there. Blood was smeared on my cheeks, but my nose was straight and no longer gushed blood. He gestured toward my steering wheel and the airbag refolded itself and molded perfectly back into the way it had been five minutes ago. I gasped.

"Just think, Macy. Think what would happen if the world could get its hands on a person who could heal in such a way," he instructed.

My mind flashed to the pool, when Jade's arms suddenly had no scrapes on them. I looked at Ahmose in alarm.

"You mean... Jade ..."

But I was talking to myself. My passenger seat was suddenly empty and I was left with a head full of questions and no one to answer them. As I looked in surprise out my window, the deer jumped easily to its feet and stared at me for a moment with clear, miraculously lucid eyes. Its legs were no longer broken and it bounded out of sight into the wooded brush next to the road.

Chapter Five

My bathroom looked like an F5 tornado had blown through it as Jade and I stood in front of the mirror getting ready for our double-date. The quartz countertops were littered with creams, ointments, cosmetics and hair products. As I spritzed spray-shine onto my hair, I glanced at Jade and found her fidgeting with her earring. She was clearly nervous.

"Calm down," I encouraged. "Seriously, Noah is nothing to be nervous about. He's gorgeous, sure, but he's got the personality of a Labrador. He likes everyone. He'll practically wag his tail when he meets you, I promise."

She smiled back and appeared just a little bit calmer. Her chestnut hair was pulled into a sleek low-ponytail and her makeup was perfect. She just needed a little pinch of color. I handed her a tube of cranberry colored lip-gloss.

"Here, this would look great on you."

She carefully applied it and I was right. It looked perfect on her. She handed it back to me.

"Thanks, Macy. Is Gavin picking Noah up... or?"

I smiled at her anxiety. This was the first time I'd ever seen her being so nervous. She had always been perfectly cool and unflustered. When she was Cleopatra, she made a point of it. She thought that anything less was 'un-queenly'.

"Yes," I answered. "And don't freak out but they should be here any minute."

As if on cue, my doorbell rang. Jade groaned and I laughed.

"You'll be fine," I assured her. "You look gorgeous."

I dragged her out by the elbow and she dropped behind as we walked to the door. I threw it open to find Gavin and Noah waiting for us with flowers.

"So, you robbed a florist on your way over?" I asked with a grin, reaching for my boyfriend and kissing him on the cheek.

"I'd do anything for you. You know that," he grinned back as he handed me the flowers.

I buried my nose in them as I introduced Noah and Jade. I noted with amusement that he did practically seem to wag his tail. He handed Jade her flowers and her eyes sparkled.

"What a gentleman," she gushed. "I love a man with manners." And that was all it took. Noah was eating out of her hand from that moment forward.

I rolled my eyes and led them in. "It'll just take a minute to put these flowers in water. Whose car do you want to take? Mine? Then we can put the top down."

"That's fine," Gavin agreed. "But let me drive. Please, by all that's holy, let me drive."

Everyone laughed and I scowled.

"Why does everyone keep teasing me about my driving?" I demanded. "I'm a great driver!"

They didn't need to know that I had crashed into a ditch yesterday. And they especially didn't need to know that I had hit a deer, killed a deer and then watched as that same deer came back to life and ran away.

Gavin rolled his eyes as he drew me in for a hug. "I know, sweetheart. You are. But can I drive anyway?"

I shook my head but relented. It didn't matter to me anyway. Jade and I hurriedly stuck our flowers in a couple of vases, grabbed our purses and we all piled into my little car. Turning around in the passenger seat, I had to laugh. My backseat was tiny and Noah was really, really large. He and

Jade were crammed together like a couple of sardines. And next to him, she looked like a tiny doll.

Gavin looked in the rearview mirror and laughed. "Maybe we should've taken my car after all."

Noah looked appalled.

"No way. I'm good." He wiggled down into the seat, which put him even closer to Jade, a fact that he obviously enjoyed.

"I bet you are," Gavin acknowledged. "So, where to? Dinner and a movie?"

"You know," I mused. "That was the plan but I'm kind of in the mood for a walk on the beach. Can we go to dinner and then maybe to Santa Monica or somewhere?"

Noah was quick to agree.

"A walk on the beach would be awesome. And Santa Monica is only an hour away. More or less." He looked at Jade. "Is that fine with you?" he asked hopefully.

She smiled her famous grin at him and I had to marvel at it. It was the same one that she had possessed when she was Cleopatra. She had charmed kings with that smile. And it was no less effective on Noah. He practically swooned into her lap as she spoke.

"Of course. That would be fun. I don't have any other place to be."

She slid her sunglasses down onto her nose and settled back into the seat. Noah tried to inconspicuously drop his arm around her shoulders, but he was about as subtle as a Mack truck. I saw her smile at the gesture and she didn't move away. Of course, to be fair, there wasn't really anywhere to go.

Gavin drove quickly to a little nearby Italian place.

"I hope you guys don't mind but I'd rather eat before we drive to Santa Monica. I'm starving."

"You're always starving," I pointed out affectionately.

"True story," he agreed. "Is this place fine with you?"

I nodded. He knew that it was. He and I came here a lot. It was tiny, quiet and out of the way. The hardwood booths were just right for intimate dates. They each had a dark stained glass lamp hanging overhead with dim lights and a candle on each table. They also had the best fresh bread in town.

I slid into a booth and Gavin scooted in beside me, pulling me up close to him. I snuggled in, dropping my head into the crook of his shoulder as I looked absently at the menu. I had been here a hundred times before. I had the thing memorized.

"Well, look what the cat dragged in," a cold voice greeted us.

I looked up to find Tara Wilson standing next to our table with an order pad in her hands. The look on her face was venomous. I felt my stomach sink into my shoes. There was no way I could order their squash-filled ravioli now. She would probably spit in it. I calmly pasted a pleasant expression on my face so that she wouldn't know that she annoyed me.

"Oh, hi, Tara. I didn't know you worked here."

"I just started last week. And I wouldn't have... if I had known that you came here."

So that was how it was going to be.

I could feel Jade's surprised gaze on my face as I met Tara's cold stare.

"Look, Tara. As far as I'm concerned, it's all water under the bridge. You're with Derek now. I'm with Gavin. There's no reason for drama. It doesn't matter anymore." I could see from her set expression that my words had fallen on deaf (or ignorant) ears.

"Sure and if you would just stop calling my boyfriend, it wouldn't matter to me anymore, either!"

I could practically feel my mouth drop open and I slowly shook my head.

"Um, I have no idea what you're talking about. I haven't called Derek in a *very* long time. He's all yours."

"You're right. He's all mine," she snarled. "Don't forget it."

She turned to Gavin. "I don't know what you're doing with Macy. You're way better than her."

He stared at her coolly. "You know, you make me forget that my mother taught me to be a gentleman."

She smiled a trashy smile at him. "Well, I could teach you lots of things that your mother can't. Call me sometime." She laid her stubby hand on his shoulder and squeezed it. I flinched.

"No, thank you," he answered, removing her hand. He edged past her and got out of the booth.

"If you guys don't mind, I don't like the atmosphere here anymore. Let's go somewhere else."

Jade quickly murmured her agreement and we all scrambled out of the booth and tried to keep up with Gavin as he strode for the car. Jade glanced over her shoulder as Tara watched us leave. As soon as we piled into the car, Jade turned to me.

"What was that all about? What did you do to her?"

"More like... what did she do to me? My ex-boyfriend cheated on me with her last year."

Her head whipped back around and she stared at me agape.

"With *that*? That's... um... insane."

"Thank you," I replied with some satisfaction. I was glad people could see how trashy she was. "It's okay. I'm way over it."

"As you should be. It's obvious that you traded up," Gavin smirked. I laughed and the mood was broken. The negative fog that Tara had brought down on us lifted.

"Come on, guys. That girl shouldn't ruin our night. Let's eat in Santa Monica, hmm?"

And with that, the tension was gone. I could hear Jade and Noah chattering in the back seat as I sat in the front, enjoying how the fall breeze blew over me. Gavin reached over and squeezed my hand and I pulled his hand up to kiss it, then held it snuggled into my lap. Being with him felt so incredibly right and it was easy to put Tara and her stupid games out of my mind. I hung my right arm over the side of the door and the hour drive passed quickly.

Instead of eating in a sit-down restaurant, we decided to grab hotdogs on the boardwalk and eat on the beach. The Pacific stretched far and wide from one side of our periphery to the other, sparkling in the evening sunlight and luring us down to the water. After we grabbed a blanket from the trunk of my car, we headed down to the beach.

"I'm not even going to ask why you have a blanket in your car," Noah laughed suggestively as he leaned around Gavin to nudge me. I shook my head.

"It's not what you're thinking. I also carry jumper-cables, water and flares. My mom insists on it. Can you say *over-protective*?" I popped him on the arm and almost lost my hot dog in the process. I recovered it and took another big bite.

"Like your little car is going to break down!" Jade rolled her eyes. "Now, my car on the other hand..."

Gavin reached over and wiped a drop of mustard from my chin, then leaned in and kissed the same spot.

"Now you're all dirty. Wanna go swimming?" he asked softly, his dark eyes gleaming in the dying sunlight. I glanced out at the choppy water. The sun was hanging on the edge of the horizon, enormous and amber. I decided that nothing was more beautiful than a sunset on the ocean right before I decided that the water was too rough to swim in. But I didn't want to admit that part.

"I don't have a suit," I pointed out primly.

"So? Swim with your clothes on. You'll dry off before we drive home," he coaxed. "Come on, you know you want to."

And I did. I had been a swimmer since the time I was small, but actually, I loved the water in every life. When I was Charmian, I swam in the bay by Alexandria, in the sparkling turquoise water of the Mediterranean. The water was soothing and warm and.... I shook myself from the memories. I was in California now.

"Well, *I* definitely would but I don't know how to swim," Noah announced.

I stared at him slack-jawed. How in the world could a big, strapping athlete like him not know how to swim? I asked him as much and he looked sheepish.

"I don't know. When I was little, my mom had this irrational fear that I would drown, so she never wanted me to learn. And as I've gotten older, I guess I just felt stupid going to swimming lessons with the five year olds!" he laughed, but quickly added, "And don't look at me like that, Lockhart. I could learn in a second, if I wanted to."

I rolled my eyes and Jade giggled, her eyes snapping.

"Prove it!" she demanded playfully. "See that buoy out there?" She pointed to a buoy two hundred yards from shore. "Swim to it."

I wondered how in the world Noah was going to get out of this one. Like most of the football players that I knew, his ego was out of control when it came to his athletic prowess. He was staring at Jade thoughtfully now, his blue eyes contemplating her.

"I could, you know," he insisted.

"Oh, we know," I interrupted. "But I want to be around to see it and right now, I want to go for a walk with my boyfriend."

"That must be my cue," Gavin drawled. "And I had just gotten comfortable. Oh, well. I'd rather stroll the beach with a beautiful girl, anyway." I reached down to help him up.

"Sorry about your luck… you'll have to settle for me."

"I know. The most beautiful girl in the world." He leaned down and kissed me on the tip of my nose.

"Ugh. Puke. Get a room!" Noah gagged. Gavin laughed.

"Come on, woman. We've got a walk to take." I froze for a moment, because that was exactly what he would have said as Hasani. And I didn't know why I was surprised. They were the same person. It was just always so startling when he said something uncanny like that. I couldn't help it.

I smiled and took his hand and we strolled along the beach barefoot. As I looked around us, it truly seemed like something out of a travel brochure. Sea gulls flew overhead, their screams filling the air. There were hardly any people here and the quiet as serene. It was perfect and something that we've done together in so many different lives.

We walked silently for awhile, enjoying the soothing crash of the ocean, before Gavin spoke.

"What do you think about Jade and Noah?"

I smiled. "I think he'll bore her to tears soon. What do you think?"

"Same. I like her, though."

"Yep, me too."

We sat down on a piece of driftwood and watched the water as he held my hand. He gazed down at me with his melted-chocolate eyes and my insides turned to mush, as the butterflies in my stomach started flying. He always had the same effect on me.

I snuggled up close. The sea breeze was just a little bit chilly as it came off the water and I shivered. He wrapped his arm around me and pulled me even closer. I melted into his warmth. And then he stiffened.

"What the hell?" he exclaimed, pointing back the way we had come.

I looked in the direction that he was pointing and immediately tensed up, both as a result of Noah's actions and the pain that was shooting from my wrist. Whatever he was doing, it was wrong, wrong, wrong. I clutched my wrist and stared.

Noah stripped off his shirt and waded into the Pacific, the pale expanse of his back reflecting the dying light of the sun. Gavin and I rushed back to where Jade was standing on the shore, all while Noah continued to walk straight out to sea. The pain from my birthmark was almost crippling.

As we got closer, Gavin shouted, "Noah, what gives?"

Noah turned around and grinned. "I'm no chicken, Chase."

"Who said you were?"Gavin shouted back.

Noah pointed at Jade and turned back around, plunging himself into the waves. I sucked in my breath. The current was known to be bad here. If an inexperienced swimmer got caught in it, it could be bad. Very bad. I grabbed Gavin's arm.

"Gavin, make him stop!"

Jade interrupted. "I didn't really mean to call him a chicken. He just started talking about swimming again and I was joking. I said, 'Well, if you ever stop being a chicken, you can put your money where your mouth is.' It wasn't a real challenge... I was *joking*." Her eyes were wide and nervous and I squeezed her elbow.

"It's not your fault. You didn't know that he could be such an idiot." I looked back out at the water. He was chest-deep now.

"Noah, get your pathetic butt back here!" I shouted. "I mean it!"

He looked at me one more time, a huge grin plastered on his face.

"You can't make me, Lockhart. You don't have *my* balls in your purse!"

He turned back around and kept walking. And then suddenly, I couldn't see him anymore. He was just gone. I gasped, gripping Gavin's arm.

"Where is he?" I cried. "Can you see him?" He had not reemerged.

Gavin pulled off his shirt and strode toward the water. Jade and I followed close on his heels. The water was cool, the tiny rocks and sand under my feet actually felt good as we waded out toward the buoy. Noah still hadn't resurfaced and I started to panic, my heart pounding loudly in my ears.

Pushing through the water, I dove under the waves and started to pull with long, strong strokes through the choppy current. The farther out I got, the murkier the water became and I couldn't see. I had to stop every few seconds to surface and look around. Gavin was directly in front of me and Jade was behind me.

And Noah was nowhere.

I reached the orange and white buoy and held onto it for a moment, bobbing with the waves as I looked around.

"Do you see him?" Gavin asked urgently, as he treaded water next to me, scanning the horizon.

"No," I answered.

But then something caught my eye and I turned back. A glint of white flashed just beneath the surface to my right.

Letting go of the buoy, I took off like a rocket. 30 seconds later, I reached it and thrust my hand under the water. I hit something fleshy and human.

"It's him!" I cried. Gavin reached me at just that moment and floating together in the waves, we turned Noah over so that his face was above the surface. His eyes were shut, his mouth was hanging open.

"Oh, god," I whispered.

"We've got to get him to shore."

Gavin was already swimming with Noah tucked under his arm. I followed, trying to help him keep Noah's body afloat. It was difficult and awkward, even swimming with the current. Noah was entirely inert. I gulped hard and tried not to panic.

As soon as we reached the shore, we stretched Noah out on the sand as Jade dropped to her knees beside us.

"This is all my fault," she wailed, grabbing Noah's hand. "He's so cold!"

"It's just from being in the water, Jade. Calm down," I instructed.

I quickly felt for a pulse and was actually surprised to find one. It was weak, but it was there. But he wasn't breathing. I pinched his nose closed and tilted his head back, blowing into his mouth.

Nothing.

I did it again. And again. And again.

Still nothing.

I watched his chest fill up with air every time I breathed into him, but he wouldn't breathe on his own. My heart started racing, pumping adrenaline throughout my body and I felt my fingertips start to tingle with it. I could hear Jade on her phone calling for an ambulance but all I could focus on was breathing into Noah.

And just when panic was really setting in, he started coughing and spewed sea water all over me. I leaned him to the side and he vomited salty water all over the sand. I took a shaky breath and slumped into Gavin, virtually collapsing with relief. My hands were shaking but the pain in my birthmark had stopped.

Noah wiped his mouth with his hand and propped himself up on his elbow.

"Lockhart, you know, if you wanted to kiss me, you could have just asked."

My relief was overwhelming and I smiled, but then just as quickly wanted to punch him in the face. Or shake him. Or shoot him. Or possibly strangle him. But I settled for just yelling at him.

"Noah! Oh my god. How could you have done that to us? You almost died. I've never seen such a stupid thing in my whole life."

Jade was sitting next to him, stroking him lightly on the back. She looked up at me.

"I'm sorry, Macy. It was my fault. I didn't realize that I was challenging him. It was stupid."

Her gorgeous eyes were watery and I stared at her in shock.

"Seriously? Um, no. You are not going to accept the blame for this. This... this was the result of his own stupidity."

"You're right," Noah answered quietly. "I'm sorry, guys. It was stupid. Sometimes I don't think things through."

"You've got that right!" I shot back. "As in *never*!"

But my anger was fading. At least he understood that he was stupid. As I simmered down, I realized that Gavin was staring at my chest. My agitation reared its head again.

"Um, hello?" I gestured to my face. "Up here, please?"

He shook his head, smiling a little. "I thought we already ascertained that I'm not a dog? I was looking for your necklace. It's not there."

My hand flew to my neck and realization hit me like a brick wall. He was right. My bloodstone was gone. I wanted to hyperventilate, but had to pretend that I was fine. Not an easy feat. My bloodstone was everything. I jumped to my feet.

"I've got to find it," I announced. "I'm sorry but that necklace is special to me and I…"

"I know," Gavin interrupted smoothly. "Calm down, sweet. Let's go find it. Jade, can you keep an eye on Noah?"

She nodded, by this time holding Noah's head in her lap. He was milking it for all it was worth. I rolled my eyes at him and he grinned back. When Jade glanced down, he quickly closed his eyes. I rolled my eyes again before heading back toward the ocean. Good grief. I had been all the way out to the buoy so my bloodstone could be anywhere. If I lost it, I couldn't imagine the consequences. The Moirae would kill me. Maybe literally.

Gavin grasped my elbow from behind. "Macy, calm down. We'll find it."

I had my doubts, but I followed him into the water.

"Let's retrace where we were, starting at the point where you found Noah," he called over his shoulder. "It probably got pulled off when we were wrestling him to shore."

I dove under the water and started combing the sea floor, coming up ever minute or so to breathe. There was pretty much everything else you could think of… broken glass, a marble, an old can, a Frisbee, a shoe… but not my necklace.

Dread formed in the very depths of my belly, but for reasons that I didn't understand, my birthmark was silent. It wasn't hurting in the slightest. Odd. I dove back under and scoured the ocean bottom again. As I patted the sand and silt with my hands, I suddenly felt something metallic and then an electrical jolt. I couldn't see through the murk, but I innately knew it was my pendant.

Closing my fingers around the chain, I shot up to the surface and the light from the sun hit my bloodstone. I breathed a long sigh of relief and clutched it tightly to my chest. Yelling to Gavin that I had found it, I headed back to shore. I crawled onto the sand and collapsed into a heap. The emotional and physical stress had drained me. I literally felt weak.

Gavin dropped next to me as I picked slimy seaweed out of my pendant's thick chain.

"I'm so glad you found it," he murmured. "I know how much you love that necklace. Here, let me fasten it for you." Before I could stop him, he reached over and pulled the pendant from my hands.

And he grew instantly still and stiff, his eyes fixated on the distant horizon, as if I was no longer even there. I knew exactly what was happening as a million expressions flitted over his face. It had happened to me a hundred times before. Fear, worry, shock, sadness... so many things took over his handsome features in a just a minute's time as the bloodstone flooded him with visions.

I overcame my horror and yanked the necklace out of his hands, turning him to face me. Out of the corner of my eye, I saw Jade and Noah approaching us and felt panicky again. They couldn't overhear whatever it was that Gavin was going to say about his visions.

"Gavin, snap out of it," I firmly instructed, grasping his hands. "Come back to me. I'm right here."

Gavin's liquid brown eyes stared worriedly at me, his dark brow knitted together in puzzlement and confusion.

"Harmonia?"

I sucked in my breath as my heart felt like it stopped beating. *Harmonia?* I stared at him for a scant second, confusion muddling my thoughts before I snapped myself out of it. Now was not the time. No matter how much I wanted to find out who Harmonia was, I could practically feel Jade and Noah's breath on my neck.

"Gavin, you've had a shock. It's okay- it's me, Macy." I cupped his face in my hands, trying to get him to focus on mine.

He stared back at me like I was an idiot.

"I know who you are," he replied. "Did I hit my head or something?"

He looked puzzled, but only by my behavior. He had apparently completely forgotten the visions... and the fact that he had just called me Harmonia. Interesting. The bloodstone must have a different effect on him than it did on me. Or the Fates were messing with me somehow. Suspicion bubbled up within me before I tampered it down. There was no use second-guessing them at the moment.

"Is everything okay over here?" Jade asked as they dropped onto the wet sand next to us.

I nodded. "Everything's great. We found my necklace, Noah didn't drown himself... this is a stellar day."

As Noah and Gavin poked and teased each other, Jade turned to me, her eyes eagle sharp.

"What was wrong with Gavin?"

Drat her super perception skills. She'd always been that way- never missing anything. Sometimes it came in handy, but more often than not, it was a pain. Like right now.

"Nothing. He got a little disoriented in the water. No big deal. The current is bad today and that makes it easy to get turned around."

"Hmm," she drawled, studying my face. "Whatever you say."

She turned to watch Noah and Gavin, who were wrestling around beside us, kicking up sand. "Well, they both certainly seem fine now," she observed. I nodded, but my thoughts had already drifted to her and the vision that I had seen of her strapped to a hospital bed. The boys were fine. But was she?

Chapter Six

$\mathscr{B}$eneath the surface of the pool, the water was a blue tinted serenity that I craved every day. I tried to stay after swim practice at least twice a week so that I could collect myself in solitude, pulling my thoughts together into something that made cohesive sense. In here, I was alone in utter silence. It was a refreshing change of pace. Nothing could bother me. Not Tara, not the Moirae, not the mysterious Keres.

I broke the surface, took a deep breath and dove back under. As I pulled with long strokes, I allowed my mind to wander. There was so much to think about. At the very top of the headache inducing questions was Harmonia. Who was she? And why was Gavin murmuring her name? I felt a brief stirring of jealousy but thought the better of it. That was ridiculous. The best part of being a soul mate was knowing that you were meant for each other.

I kicked off the tiled wall and shot toward the other side of the pool, plunging my face once again into the cold water. And immediately startled, flailing for a moment before I regained my composure.

Directly in front of me, about ten yards away in the deep end, Ahmose was floating in the depths of the pool like a giant black jellyfish, watching me with an intense expression on his creepy face. His black robes were floating all around him and his long gnarled limbs were stretched toward me in an ominous, fear-inducing presence. So much for being alone.

Macy, we need to talk.

I heard his thoughts immediately in my mind, as clearly as if he had spoken aloud.

Quickly. Time is of the essence.

I scowled at him as I swam to the side of the pool and pulled myself up and over the ledge, dripping on the tiles. I glanced around me. No one else was here. Thank god.

Ahmose shot through the surface of the water, spraying me with chlorinated droplets, then lightly landed on his feet next to me. He was completely dry- as though he'd never been submerged at all.

"Why must you persist in scaring me to death?" I asked him in agitation. "Would it really be so hard to just walk up to me like a normal human being?"

He stared down his long nose at me and I could practically feel the tension in his ancient body. The air around us was pregnant with it which immediately put me on edge.

"As much as I would like to engage in conversation with you, Macy, I don't have the time. Things are spiraling out of control and there isn't time to elaborate."

Alarm filled me up and every bit of me became panicked. Ahmose never allowed himself to be flustered. Until now. I gulped. I started to shake and I knew it had less to do with being soaking wet and more to do with this unknown situation.

"What do you mean?" I asked hesitantly.

"Listen to me, Keeper, and listen well. I don't have the time to repeat myself. Trust no one. Do you understand?" I stared at him in shock and he rasped again, impatient.

"Do you understand?" he persisted, his voice harsh. I nodded.

"Why are you telling me this? What is going on?"My voice was thin and I could hear the uncertainty in it. So could he and he shook his head.

"I can't explain. I wish that I could, but I have been rendered mute by the Moirae on this topic. I literally cannot speak of it. But there are things you still need to know." He trailed off and studied me with his intense glittering eyes.

"Such as?" I pressed.

"I cannot say. But I can show you what I have seen... what you don't remember."

I sucked in my breath. "I don't know that I want to do that. It makes everything too hard."

He hissed, a scary rasping noise that snapped my teeth together.

"Come here. I care not about what you *want*. I know what you *need*."

I took one tentative step towards him and held my hand out. I could see my fingertips shake as I waited for him to grasp them. The second he curled his gnarled fingers around mine, I was immediately immersed in his memories.

Just as though I was looking through his eyes, I stood in the middle of an ancient city. I glanced down at my feet and found his black robes swirled around his bare, crooked toes. I was standing on the edge of a circular arena with white marble columns all around me. I was in a coliseum of some sort. And I was not alone.

In the middle of the ring, standing in the powdery dust, was a woman and a man. They stood calmly holding hands, clearly waiting for something. The woman had long, dark hair that flowed to the middle of her back and I grew instantly still. It was me. I knew it even before she turned her head and I saw her jade green eyes. She stared quietly at the man, who returned her stare with a dark, smoldering gaze. Gavin. I would know him anywhere. My heart stopped beating as I watched a third person approach them from the opposite side of the arena.

The man was very large, very intimidating and had wild hair. Like Gavin and I, he was dressed as an ancient Greek. His toga was shimmering grayish silver and as he reached where

Gavin and I stood, it glimmered in the light. As he spoke, his eyes flashed silver as well. I cringed. His voice was like thunder. It literally rattled my bones.

"Cadmus, you killed Ares' dragon. You served him loyally for years. You've been the King of Thebes. You have your lovely wife by your side." The man paused to stare at us for a moment before continuing.

"Yet you are unhappy. You wish to leave all that you know behind."

Gavin visibly tightened his grip on me and nodded solemnly.

"We do. Our children have met with such tragedy. We do not wish to remain. Please allow it to be so, great Zeus. It is all we ask, now that you have so kindly accommodated our other wish." I watched as I nodded quietly, in perfect agreement. *Zeus? This couldn't be real.*

Zeus, who looked exactly like every depiction that I've ever seen of him, seemed to consider the request for a moment before finally nodding.

"Very well. Let it be so. You will not be bothered with troubles from our world again."

He lifted a heavy staff and pounded it into the dirt. It landed so hard that the earth trembled and great clouds of dust exploded into the air. I frantically tried to see through the haze but it took a few seconds to clear. When it settled, Gavin and I were no longer standing in the arena. In our places, two long snakes lay stretched out on the ground. I gasped.

"Now it is so," Zeus muttered and spun around, walking quickly away.

The snakes started moving, slithering toward me. *No, no, NO.*

I yanked my hand from Ahmose's grasp and immediately the vision ended. I was safely back on the pool deck. I took a step toward the priest and opened my mouth speak, but closed it. What in the world should I say? I had no idea where to begin. I settled on the obvious.

"What the hell was that?"I demanded. My voice shook though and I knew he heard it.

"That is who you are," Ahmose stated simply. I stared at him and waited for the layers of confusion to fall away as usually happened when he showed me a vision. But it didn't happen. Old memories didn't reemerge.

"Where are my memories? Why haven't they returned?"

"Because they have been blocked very thoroughly. And I am not allowed to give them to you. I must go and it is likely you will not see me again, Keeper. Find Annen. Listen to what he says to you."

"You told me to ignore him!" I gasped. "You said that he was lying."

"I know what I said. And it was necessary at the time. But I'm telling you now. Find him."

"Someone cut his tongue out..." I trailed off and Ahmose nodded.

"Yes. There is much at stake here and truthfully, we are all in danger. I don't know if we will survive it."

"You're scaring me," I replied, staring into his eyes.

"I mean to. Trust no one, watch behind you."

And he was gone. I stood in a puddle of water on the slippery tiles staring into thin air where he had just been two seconds ago. I grabbed my towel and rubbed it vigorously up and down my arms, trying to restore the blood flow that had been stopped with his chilling words.

Something was terribly wrong. I had been aware of it for days, but now it was confirmed. If Ahmose was scared, then I should be too.

* * *

I couldn't get home fast enough, even with my typical pedal-to-the-metal driving style. I barricaded myself in my room and flew to my desk, booting up my laptop. I had one name to go on. *Cadmus.* Gavin had been Cadmus. I quickly punched that into a search engine and a myriad of results popped up. After five minutes, I sat back in my chair completely dumbfounded.

Cadmus had been the King of Thebes, just as Zeus mentioned in my vision. He had angered the Greek god Ares by killing his dragon and was forced to serve him for several years. After he loyally served the time assigned to him, he was rewarded by being given a bride. Harmonia, the daughter of Aphrodite and Ares himself. *Me.*

Time seemed to stand still as I flew through the other websites, reading a mile a minute, my eyes quickly absorbing every bit of information that I could drudge up.

At their wedding (my wedding!) Harmonia and Cadmus were given a gift by Harmonia's stepfather. But it wasn't just any gift. Her stepfather, Hephaestus, had been harboring bitter feelings toward his wife, Aphrodite. Apparently, Harmonia (me!) had been conceived with Ares. Aphrodite had been cheating on her husband with the god of war. To get his revenge, Hephaestus appealed to Zeus and had created a beautiful necklace for Harmonia as a wedding gift. It was made with Zeus' own blood. And it had been cursed.

Any wearer of the necklace would retain her beauty and youth, but she would suffer great misfortune. One of Harmonia's own daughters met a violent end because of it. After their children suffered so much, Harmonia and Cadmus were turned into snakes and sent to the fields of Elyria to live for the rest of eternity. The necklace was passed to Queen Jocasta and after her husband died, she married her own son,

Oedipus. When the world discovered his identity, he scratched his own eyes out and she killed herself.

I felt numb. My necklace had created the Oedipus complex.

My necklace. I fingered the bloodstone that was lying against my chest. It was cool against my skin, even through my shirt. It couldn't be the same necklace. Could it? Lachesis had told me that there were twelve Keepers and each of us had a necklace. Harmonia's Necklace was only one.

"Cadmus," I whispered, testing the name out on my tongue.

It felt right. Obviously it was an old, old name and it should feel that way to me.... Antiquated. But it didn't. It formed on my tongue as though it was meant to be there. Probably because it was. Cadmus was Gavin and I was a goddess. But if we had been sent to Elyria for eternity, then what was I doing here now? Why had I been acting as a Keeper of Fate for so many millennia?

My mind was spinning. This was too much craziness for any one person to handle without ice cream. I padded into the kitchen for some chocolate chip banana therapy. I didn't even bother with a bowl, I just sat with a spoon and the ice cream carton. As I ate, I stared at my hands, my arms, my legs, the way my hair curled around my shoulder. It felt so odd to know that I had been around for thousands of years and that apparently I was a goddess. But now I was human.

What had happened in the meantime to put me here? I had no idea. But I knew someone who did. Annen.

I set aside the ice cream and picked up my bloodstone, silently willing Annen to appear.

Nothing.

I pleaded.

Nothing.

I sighed.

Still nothing.

I gave up and put my dirty dishes in the sink and returned to my bedroom before my mom got home. I loved my mom like crazy, but I wasn't in the mood for chit-chat. There was so much to figure out. I started in the most logical place of all.

I dialed Gavin's number and felt a rush of relief when his husky voice flooded into my phone.

"Hey, beautiful," he answered.

"Hey," I sighed, settling back into the pillows of my bed. "Want to come over?" I asked hopefully.

If anything could help me right now, it would be him. Seeing his familiar face, holding his hand... it would make everything better. I knew it. Out of all the craziness in all of my lives, he had always been a constant. Well, he and Ahmose. And Ahmose said that I might not see him again. Cryptic words. I sighed again.

"What's wrong?" Gavin asked. He knew me so well.

"Nothing. I just miss you."

"I wish I could come over. But I've got to cram for that stupid history final tomorrow."

Gavin was regretful and I instantly recognized the humor in this situation. I was a goddess and Gavin had been the King of Thebes, slayer of dragons. And here we were in Pasadena worrying about high school. What kind of hell was this?

"It's okay," I replied softly. "Hearing your voice is almost as good."

"Macy, what is wrong with you?" He sounded so concerned that it warmed my heart. "Did your dad call or something?"

"No," I answered. "I haven't heard from him in weeks. Nothing's wrong. Really. I just wanted to see you. I'll see you tomorrow though. Want to pick me up for school?"

"Of course I do. I want to make sure you get there in one piece. I love you, you know."

"I know. I love you, too."

I hung up the phone and laid it gently on the bed stand. Gazing around my room, I just couldn't bring myself to do homework. That was just too trivial with everything else going on. Crossing the room, I grabbed my laptop and returned to my bed. Some thorough research of my ancestry was in order, beginning with my father. My real father. Ares, the god of war.

Hours passed. I heard my mother come home and barely lifted my head when she asked if I wanted any dinner. Thankfully, she left me alone the rest of the evening while she had a movie night with a friend. My eyes had begun to burn from so much online reading by the time I finally closed the lid to my laptop. I lay quietly staring at the wall, pondering my new history. My true and original history.

My thoughts flew back to Alexandria when I had saved Hasani's (Gavin's…Cadmus'…) life. At the time I had no idea how I had done it. Strength from within me had just exploded into that cave and the next thing I knew, Hasani was opening his eyes. It had to be because of who I was… not because of the bloodstone at all, which is what I had thought at the time.

I had the blood of a goddess. A minor goddess, but still. A goddess was a goddess. It was a fact that kept running through my mind until the very minute that sleep overtook me.

* * *

I was surrounded in blackness. I stared around, frantically trying to get my bearings. A minute ago I had been in the safety of my bed and now I was elsewhere. A dream. A dream? Was I dreamwalking again?

I was in a long, musty stone hallway. I heard raspy whisperings floating from the end of it, so I felt along the stone wall to find where it was coming from. Oddly enough, even though I wasn't physically here, I could feel the dampness beneath my fingers as I crept along. It was also so black that I couldn't see a foot in front of my face. Frustrating. My bare foot slid into something furry and moving and I fought back a scream. Whatever it was scurried away from me and I breathed a sigh of relief.

I approached the end of the hall and I found myself facing a door. Light seeped from under it and I edged closer cautiously. Silently, I opened it just a little and peered inside. The first thing I noticed were a thousand candles floating throughout the room from ceiling to floor. Their soft glow surrounded three cloaked figures and Ahmose.

But Ahmose is who held my attention.

The ancient priest was suspended in mid-air, his face contorted in agony. I couldn't see what they were doing to him—their hands were not physically on him, but he was obviously in excruciating pain. He writhed and turned in mid-air, but stubbornly refused to even whimper. I could clearly see though, the effort that it cost him. Sweat poured in rivulets from his forehead and his jaw was clenched tightly closed. A tiny muscle in his cheek ticked as he stared down at his attackers.

"You dared to defy us?" A hissing voice asked and I closed my eyes. There was so much malice in the voice that the mere sound of it scared me. I felt my thighs tremble as I hovered quietly outside the door. I couldn't stand not knowing, though, so I opened my eyes again.

Ahmose remained silent, hanging limply in the air like a long, black dishtowel.

"Answer me!" the voice hissed and Ahmose straightened his body out with a harsh groan. Clearly, they were torturing him somehow. Mental agony? It was though he was stretched on an invisible rack. I could tell each time they inflicted pain on him only by the way he held his body.

"I did what was right," he muttered limply, as his body slumped once again. A thin stream of blood flowed out of his ear and dripped onto his dark robes and I flinched.

"How dare you think you can decide what is right!" another hooded figure asked venomously.

There were three of them. Like the Fates. But their voices were not familiar. The Keres? They were small and hunched, but apparently lethal. I frantically tried to decide what to do, but ultimately, I knew that there was nothing. I wasn't physically here.

I peered into the room once again and this time, found Ahmose staring directly at me, his black eyes drilling into mine. I clasped a hand over my mouth and his gaze never faltered. It was as though he was piercing my soul with it. I knew, in that moment, that he had summoned me here. He wanted me to witness this. For that reason only, I forced my eyes to remain open.

His feet were shaking, probably from pain, as he dangled like a rag doll in the air. Blood was seeping from the corners of his eyes now, as well as his ear and I desperately wanted to turn away, but his gaze held me immobilized.

"You will not win," he finally uttered to them with great effort. "She won't allow it."

The three figures huddled around him and then stepped backward.

"But we will," the figure replied. "She can't stop us."

And with that, Ahmose dropped from the air into a heap on the floor and instantly exploded into flames. His torturous screams filled the room and my heart as I turned away.

I sat straight up in bed with a gasp. Relieved, I looked around me. I was home. Safe and sound. I had no idea where I had just been, but I was so happy to be here now. I tried to calm my frantic breathing as my heart pounded against my sternum like a runaway freight train.

And then I saw him.

Someone was standing in the corner of my room, outlined by the silvery light of the moon. Tall and thin, his pale face was luminescent in the shadows. My pulse picked up again. I didn't take my eyes off of him as I leaned to turn on my lamp. Before I could even reach the switch, he was standing directly in front of me, his ice-cold hand wrapped around my arm. He was lightening fast.

"Don't," he instructed, his breath so cold that it I could see it in the warm air.

"Why?" I whispered, staring into his silvery eyes.

"Walk with me," he answered. He motioned to me and I was instantly on my feet, although I had not actually moved a muscle.

He grasped my elbow lightly, like a perfect gentleman, guiding me toward the door. Gavin did this very same thing sometimes, in a crowded room. But this icy grip was certainly not Gavin's and it wasn't comforting in the slightest.

We walked through the dark house to the back door and out to the quiet pool. Moonlight reflected off of the still water and I could smell the chlorine on the breeze along with the honeysuckle on the side of the house. Comforting, familiar scents in a terrifying situation.

He led me to a nearby chair and gestured for me to sit. I did so, then looked up at him.

"Who are you?"

"Alexi," he replied. He didn't smile, nor did he scowl. He simply had an expressionless face.

"And why are you here? Why were you in my room in the middle of the night?" I asked, getting back a little of my feistiness. Who did he think he was?

"I think you know why, Harmonia."

My breath froze in my throat.

"You know who I am?" I asked nervously, glancing around.

"Of course. As do you… and therein lies the problem."

Chapter Seven

Aexi stared at me, his gaze sharp and unwavering. I tried not to flinch. *Do not let him see your fear. Do not let him see it.* I chanted it in my head like a mantra while I clenched my fists tightly. He smiled, an eerily haunting gesture that flooded my entire body with white-hot fear.

"I can read your mind, my dear," he stated, studying me calmly. "I know that you are afraid."

"Who are you?" I whispered. "Did the Moirae send you?"

"Of course," he confirmed, so emotionless and matter-of-fact. "As you just saw, Ahmose is, shall we say, permanently indisposed. You are in need of a new Aegis."

"Yet, you're not an Aegis," I pointed out, trying not to think about poor Ahmose.

"They told me you were smart," he observed sarcastically, right before he blurred into motion.

In a movement as quick as hummingbird wings, he bent and grasped my elbow and pulled me to his side. His icy fingers had barely touched me before I was standing limply once again.

"Come with me," he murmured.

With his free hand, he gestured toward the pool and as I watched in amazement, the water began to churn around in a whirlpool-like frenzy. It quickly developed such power that it sloshed over the sides of the pool deck in frothy, white splatters. He lifted his hand and the water followed it, swirling up into a funnel, emptying the pool as the water hovered in the air above us, still spiraling like a tornado. I gasped and stared at him as he turned slowly to face me.

"After you," he said, gesturing toward the pool steps. The empty pool seemed scary to me now, particularly with the water that was supposed to be in it hanging above my head.

Nervously, I descended the stairs with him, allowing him to lead me down the slanted tiles until we were standing in the empty deep end. The tiled walls surrounding me seemed cavernous and the water hung over our heads like a furious cloud, churning silently. I glanced up at it and felt my pulse race against my birthmark. But no pain. Oddly, even with this clearly out of the ordinary experience, my tell-tale birthmark remained silent. I grasped it anyway and waited, holding my breath as I watched Alexi, waiting for his next movement.

He lowered his arm and the water came crashing down. I cringed and braced for the impact as I felt it graze against the top of my head.

And we were gone.

We were suddenly standing in clouds. I shook my head to clear it, to try and gain my bearings amid my overwhelming confusion.

Wispy clouds clung to my arms and legs as we stood in front of a great iron gate. White marble columns stood on each side of it, topped with giant, terrifying falcons. They were so enormously large that they seemed to be the size of mountain lions. And they were not stone. They were alive. Their eyes were blood red, their expressions fierce. As I moved, so did their heads, following me with their crimson eyes. I shivered.

"Open the gates," Alexi commanded. "Harmonia is here to see the Moirae."

The falcon on the left opened its beak. "Answer the question first, then you may pass, servant."

Alexi's grip tightened on my elbow and I could feel his agitation seeping through his fingertips. Apparently, he didn't enjoy being referred to as a servant.

"I do not answer to you," he replied through gritted teeth. "I come bearing Harmonia. Deny us entrance and the Sisters will be angry."

The falcons watched him with identical bored expressions, each tilting their heads just a little to the left. Light glistened off of their iridescent feathers and I realized that tiny shards of gold were embedded within their plumes. They turned to me, identical and terrifying, their massive talons curled around the platforms on which they sat.

"Harmonia, how long must one wander the shores of Hades if the boatman isn't paid?" The falcon closest to me rasped.

"One hundred years," I answered promptly.

And then I gasped. I would never get used to having subconscious knowledge and memories surface at random moments. I could suddenly see an image of the river Styx in my head as clearly as if I were standing in front of it. Murky, turbulent water wound its way to the gates of Hades with lost souls wandering on each side. It was a dark, unhappy place and I shook my head to free myself of the memory.

"Correct," the bird uttered as they both nodded in unison. "You may enter, but remember to drink from the cup."

The heavy gates swung open and the birds dipped their heads in deference as I passed beneath them. Alexi followed directly on my heels. I could almost feel his glacial breath on my neck. Confused by the falcon's dictate, I turned to face Alexi.

"Drink from the cup?"

He nodded curtly toward a golden table sitting directly inside the gates beneath a small, blossoming tree. Magnificent blue flowers dropped from the branches every few minutes and landed in a basket on the ground. On the table, a jeweled goblet was sitting in the shade. Alexi nudged me toward it.

"Drink from the cup."

I eyed it suspiciously. "What is it?"

He gave me a droll look. "Does it matter? If you don't drink, you cannot continue into Olympus. And if you do not appear in front of the Sisters, they will kill you. Drink."

"Can you not just tell me what it is?" I asked in exasperation. Why did everything need to be so difficult?

"It is nectar," he replied brusquely. "Now, drink it."

I picked up the heavy golden chalice, wrapping my fingers around the solid stem and sniffed at the clear liquid within. It had the consistency of thick syrupy juice but was transparent like water. It had a heavy, sweet smell unlike anything I'd encountered before- a mixture of peaches, mangoes, cherries... I couldn't put my finger on it. I hesitated, even though the smell was rapidly drawing me in. I felt an incredible compulsion to drink.

Alexi smiled a superior, knowing smile.

"You've drunk from this cup a thousand times before. It will not harm you. Drink." He motioned with his hand and I gathered up my courage. I could do this.

I sipped tentatively at the liquid, but it was so overwhelmingly delicious and fragrant that I forgot myself and tipped the cup back, draining every ounce of the sweet goodness, gulping so fast that it streaked down my chin. As I finished the last swallow, I wiped at my face with my hand. Glancing down, I gasped again.

My hand was covered in blood.

Holding the goblet up so that I could peer into the reflection, I saw in horror that my chin and teeth were smeared with crimson streaks. I looked like an evil, blood-drinking fiend.

"What is the nectar made from?" I turned to Alexi in a panic with wide eyes.

"The blood of the unborn," he answered. "You know this. It gives you eternal life."

I fell onto my knees, gagging as I coughed. But even as I did, the revulsion quickly faded, replaced with a strange feeling unlike anything I remembered. It began in my toes and quickly worked itself up like an invisible presence. It was.... Knowledge. Understanding. Power. Awareness. Clarity. Harmonia's memories returned in a scant blink of an eye. I was her. She was me.

Harmonia. Visions of my life as Harmonia, flew into my memory with startling speed.

I stopped coughing and slowly rose from the ground, standing with my shoulders back and my chin up. I felt my face literally tighten as I stood. I knew I was losing the baby fat that Macy still carried in her cheeks as I acquired Harmonia's more adult face. I wanted to look, but didn't have time. I would do it later.

"There we go," Alexi approved. "Gratitude for being quick."

I threw him a look as I walked ahead of him. He knew his place was behind me. And now so did I. I could feel my sense of entitlement as a goddess, as the daughter of Aphrodite and Ares, returning to me. I wasn't sure I liked it. There were certain things that were done simply because of who I was yet there wasn't anything I could do but accept it.

"Why have I been summoned here?" I asked Alexi.

As I did, I looked around me. Mount Olympus was in ruins. It was still beautiful with winding paths, ancient marble buildings and magnificent gardens, but everything was crumbling and in disrepair. Diaphanous clouds drifted around us and the air smelled like heaven...wisteria, jasmine, honeysuckle. I recalled that Olympus was specifically beautiful to each beholder, meaning it was beautiful to each inhabitant in a different way, each person's own perception of perfection.

Just like my mother. Aphrodite had the same gift. It was why her smile was so charming.

I glanced through the drifting clouds to stare at Alexi.

"Why am I here?" I repeated.

"Because they wanted you here," he answered. "And we need to move. They don't like to wait."

He grasped my arm again and propelled me forward and we moved fluidly throughout the beautiful, aging city. As I looked around, I found minor gods and goddesses like myself, but not any of the Olympic gods. Aphrodite, Ares, Zeus, Hera... None of the twelve were here.

"Where is Zeus?" I asked. Zeus was an overwhelming presence on Mount Olympus. You could feel him long before you could see him. He was the personification of the word *Intimidating*.

Alexi stared at me silently, his lips pressed together in a thin line.

"You ask quite a few questions for someone in your precarious position," he remarked.

"What exactly is my position?" I asked. "Why have I been cast into a mortal's body? It doesn't make sense."

"It will," he promised. "Soon."

We continued our stroll through Olympus and I continued to gawk around me. The once magnificent homes were crumbling, but still beautiful in a sad way. In fact, there was a general air of solemn sadness all around me. Normally, faint music was audible all throughout Olympus. Not so now. There were no harps or flutes, no dancing nymphs. I was instantly on edge.

A few minutes later, we stood at the base of Zeus' palace. The enormous building was dark and quiet, its windows staring at me like a thousand pairs of blank eyes. I could feel someone watching me, but I couldn't see them. It was unsettling.

We climbed the stone steps and I heard rustling from behind me, but when I turned, there was no one there. I shook my head and kept walking. When we got to the top, I found Hephaestus chained to a post by the door. My step-father was wearing a dog-like harness which was attached to a chain. He sat hunched over until we approached.

He lumbered to his feet, favoring his lame leg. Both of his legs were crippled, but one troubled him more than the other. He glanced at me briefly before opening the doors for us.

"You've kept them waiting," he stated.

I stared at him aghast, utterly baffled.

"Hephaestus, you're their doorman?! A god such as yourself has been reduced to wearing a dog's collar? What is the meaning of this? What is going on?"

He stared at me bleakly, his dark eyes empty.

He sighed heavily and replied, "You don't know how lucky you are to have received your fate. Anything is preferable to this. I didn't know when I made your necklace what was to become of it. And to us."

He pushed the door open with a thick arm and stood to the side to allow us to pass. I couldn't help but stare at him as we passed, the foreboding feelings building up to a crescendo in my chest. There was no way that this was good.

Inside the palace, it looked like a frat party had trashed the place. Priceless bits of history were strewn about. I could see Achilles' shield propped in a corner and gasped. It should be guarded. It was impenetrable, making it incredibly desirous to have. Yet it was discarded in the corner like an unwanted trinket. What was going on here?

Alexi led me to the courtyard behind the palace and I willingly followed, eager to make sense out of this whole thing. Apparently, only three people could explain it. The Moirae.

They sat with their backs to me in black marble chairs in the sun. As I approached, Lachesis spoke.

"You had so much promise, Harmonia, yet you've disappointed us so greatly."

She turned slowly in her seat and I sucked my breath in.

She was ancient. Her wrinkles were deep and creviced, her eyes faded. She lifted a gnarled finger and motioned for me to come closer. Once upon a time, she had appeared as a beautiful woman to me, because she hadn't wished to scare me. Apparently, that was no longer her concern.

I swallowed hard and walked to her, having no idea at what was to come.

Clothos and Atropos stared on silently, each as terrifying as Lachesis. As I got closer to Atropos, my life force began to appear around me, clinging to my body. She leaned forward and inhaled just a little, as though she was sampling it. It wafted toward her like a magnet and she sucked at it a little, then blew it back at me. I tried not to hyperventilate. With a single breath, she could kill me.

She grinned a toothless grin at me and I shuddered.

"Sister," Clothos cautioned, and Atropos sat back in her seat. She looked disappointed that her fun had been thwarted.

"You are a thorn in my side," Clothos reprimanded me. "You have one duty and one duty only now. To protect your Daedal. Yet she's been threatened on your watch. Your Aegis has been punished in your stead. And you have been granted a new one. Don't abuse it this time."

Her faded blue eyes appraised me and I squirmed, then summoned my inner feistiness.

"Clothos, please explain what is going on. Where is Zeus? Where are my parents? You have much to explain."

She laughed, condescending and amused at once.

"As if you can demand that, Keeper. You can no longer command as a goddess, have you not noticed? Look around you. Olympus belongs to us. Which means you do, as well. Behave and we will spare Cadmus."

Cadmus. *Gavin.* My heart lurched in my chest and I tried to show no outward signs of alarm, but they could read me like a book. They had access to my thoughts and Clothos could taste my emotions, yet another gift. She licked her lips and swallowed.

"Terror is so delicious," she remarked. "You're disappointingly predictable, Harmonia. All these years and you would still risk everything for him. Tsk,tsk. Your father would be ashamed."

"Where *is* my father?" I inquired politely, trying to keep my voice steady.

"Not here," she replied mysteriously. "Ares can't help you."

"What is your obsession with my Daedal? Why is she so important?" I asked. "Surely, if I am to protect her, you should tell me why she is important. It would help."

They seemed to consider it for a moment before Lachesis replied.

"She possesses a… gift. It is in the best interest of mortals to discover this gift."

"Is it the Keres who want to stop that?" I asked.

"Yes. It is the Keres. You love your precious humans so much that you should want to help them, no?" Atropos asked. "The Keres want to kill your Daedal. You must prevent that."

"What is her gift?"

"That will be revealed in due time, Keeper," Lachesis said. "It is not of your concern at the moment."

"She can heal… very quickly. Is that her gift? Why would the Keres want to kill her for that reason? It doesn't make sense."

"Surely you are not questioning us," Clothos inquired steadily.

"No. I am just trying to figure it out."

Clothos laughed, a chilling sound.

"Harmonia, you've never changed. You see the very best in people, not what they are actually capable of."

Her mention of my name reminded me of a more important issue to press.

"Clothos, why have I been rendered mortal? Where is everyone else? How have you managed to do this?"

All three sisters cackled at that, their ancient faces twisted and ugly. I flinched.

"Do we repulse you?" Atropos asked, sitting forward in her chair. She seemed eager and I instantly shook my head.

"No, of course not. I'm just confused. That is all. Why have you done this?"

Clothos sobered and stared at me. "You've never known what it is like to have a father who doesn't claim you. You were a bastard daughter yet Ares proudly claimed you as his. Our own father never publicly announced us, even though we were so valuable to him. He only loved us for our gifts."

"I'm sure that Zeus meant no harm…" I began, but she interrupted sharply.

"He meant exactly what he did, to shun us for centuries. He has gotten his just desserts."

I swallowed, stared at the bitter women and then swallowed again. How did one go about arguing with insanity?

"But what about everyone else?" I asked. "What did they do to deserve this?"

"Mainly nothing," Lachesis shrugged. "But no one ever stepped in. For instance, Hera could have easily insisted to her husband that he do the right thing, but she did not."

"But it is no one else's fault," I protested. "I'm sure they meant no harm."

"As do we. We mean no harm. They're all being taught a valuable lesson. Humility. They need to realize that they are not as important as they think."

"Where are they?" I asked again, hoping that they might change their minds and tell me. But no such luck. Atropos was already shaking her ancient head.

"No, dear Keeper. That shall remain our secret for now."

Clothos turned back to me, her faded eyes becoming fierce. My stomach tightened.

"You need to concern yourself with guarding your Daedal. Make sure that the Keres do not get close to her. If they do..." she stopped speaking as Atropos leaned forward, inhaling ever so gently against my life force. It pulled toward her slightly and I took a step back. She laughed, a malevolent, eerie sound.

"If they do, I'll let Atropos finish," Clothos confirmed.

I nodded.

"I've come to love my Daedal," I replied. "Of course I wish no harm to come to her, so I will do my best to guard her. Can you tell me.... When will you allow the other gods to return home?" My gaze swept below the palace toward the ravaged streets of Olympus before I returned my attention to the Fates.

"They deserve to come home, sisters."

Lachesis cocked her head, her white hair curled around her thin shoulders.

"That will probably never happen, but I should probably never say never," she replied cryptically. She smiled, amused at her own vagueness.

"Harmonia, this situation is unlike anything you've seen before. You will need to take on the role of protector, which will require you to use your gifts. Harmonia's gifts. That is the reason you were called here today. You have drunk from the cup, which has returned your gifts to you. For now. Over the coming days, you'll feel... more yourself. Use caution," she instructed.

I nodded. It was true. I already felt different than before. I felt... awake. That was the best way to put it. I felt as though I had been asleep before and now I had been awakened. Something that I couldn't explain pulsed through my veins and it both alarmed me and excited me. It felt as though I was home. Because I was.

"Yes," I agreed. "I will use caution."

"Do your job well, and we will consider allowing your parents to return," Clothos mentioned casually and I startled. I knew she was lying, but the knowledge that whatever Jade was was so important that she would bother to lie was alarming. What in the hell *was* she?

"That will be all," Clothos dismissed me and they all promptly turned their backs on me again. I stood uncertainly until Alexi grasped my elbow once more and led me back out through the palace.

As we passed Hephaestus, I glanced over my shoulder to find him staring at me. His eyes were pensive and soulful and I wondered what he was thinking. Did he think I could help? And why would I want to help him anyway, after he had tried to curse me for all of eternity? Yet, I couldn't help but admit that I felt sorry for him. His great shoulders slumped and he sat once more next to the post he was chained to.

We stopped directly before the massive gates at the small golden table. Alexi motioned toward the basket of blue blossoms.

"You must eat one," he instructed.

I stared at him suspiciously. "Why? What are they? The bones of the unforgiven?"

"Don't be silly," he replied. "They are simply Lotus Blossoms... one of the many forms of ambrosia. You must eat one to return to the mortal world."

I stared at him once more before approaching the basket hesitantly. As I drew nearer, just as the nectar had lured me in with its delicious smell, so too did the blossoms. Their sweet smell drifted to me on the breeze and it was almost hypnotic. I knelt by the basket and pulled one out with trembling fingers, raising the fragrant flower to my lips. I ate it quickly, savoring the rich flavor. It was the most delicious thing I had ever eaten.

I felt slightly woozy as I stood and faced Alexi.

"Now what?"

He took my arm and we strolled out, the falcons above us strangely quiet as they observed us. As soon as we stepped from the gates, they swung closed with a metallic clang. We were once again surrounded by clouds, but through them, I saw that we were standing on a steep precipice. I could see the ground hundreds of miles below us. I inhaled sharply as I turned to Alexi.

"How do we get back?"

"Like this," he replied. He grasped my arm yet again and we stepped from the edge.

And I was in my bed. I had no recollection of falling from the edge of Mount Olympus at all. I simply stepped from the edge and then suddenly, I was here... in the dark safety of my room. Alexi was gone.

I glanced at my clock. 3:00 a.m. My breaths were shaky and nervous and I consciously tried to still them. Reaching for my bed stand, I grabbed my phone.

Gavin would be asleep, but I needed to tell him that I loved him. More than ever, I realized that it had always been him. He had always been the most important thing. My fingers flew as I typed the text.

I love you more than life.

When he woke up in the morning, he would wonder why I had sent him such a sentimental text at 3:00 in the morning. Honestly, I just needed to be close to him. This all seemed like a horrible dream. I clasped my phone to my chest and closed my eyes, willing myself to sleep.

Chapter Eight

$\mathscr{I}$ woke to persistent whining and opened my eyes. Early morning light streamed through my bedroom windows and I blinked, trying to place the noise that had woken me. It whined again.

I glanced down and found Hamlet cowering next to me, trying to crawl under my bed. He was too large, so only his head was buried beneath my bed frame. His entire body was shaking as he whimpered. I reached down and patted him.

"What's the trouble, Hammie?" I murmured, trying to soothe him as I forced myself to wake up.

He whimpered again.

And the house started to shake. Right in front of my eyes, my bedroom walls seemed to flex, then tremble as my bed lurched. I could hear glass breaking somewhere else in the house and Hamlet gave up trying to get under my bed and instead lunged into bed with me. My bedside table vibrated away from the bed, the lamp crashing to the floor.

The drawers on my tall dresser slid out, the weight causing the entire dresser to tumble over. Every one of the glass globes that my dad had been giving me for years flew off. I watched one shatter against the wall, the glittery liquid inside running down in streaks.

After a moment, the heavy rumbling stopped, leaving behind only sporadic quivers. Aftershocks. I took a deep breath, rubbing Hammie's soft ears.

"It's okay, boy," I consoled him. "It's over now. We should be used to this." But we weren't. It was always startling.

My mom barged into my room, stepping around my fallen dresser and eyeing the damage.

"Are you okay?" she asked nervously. "God, I hate those things."

"Me too," I agreed. "But I'm fine. My snow globes are all broken though."

She knelt down and surveyed the mess as I untwisted myself from my blankets and the dog.

"Not this one!"

She held up one lone survivor. A delicate globe that my father had brought me from a business trip to New York. The Statue of Liberty stood proudly in the middle, holding up her torch. I had gotten it when I was eight, back when my dad was still my hero.

I crossed the room and took it from her, sitting on the edge of my bed. She sat beside me, wrapping her arm around my shoulders. I leaned my head against her, inhaling her familiar perfume.

"Speaking of your father, honey, I've been trying to get a hold of him. I have a dentistry conference this weekend and I wanted you to spend the weekend at his house. But he hasn't returned my calls yet. Maybe he's out of the country on business."

Or maybe he just doesn't give a fig, I thought. But I didn't say it. It pained my mother to no end that he had lost all interest in me. And it pained me too. I couldn't figure out if it bothered him so much that he wasn't a big part of my life anymore that he just didn't want to remind himself of that by hearing the details of my life, or if he actually just didn't care.

Surprisingly, even with Harmonia's memories returned to me, my mortal memories still bothered me. My mortal father could still cause me pain. Curious. I turned to my mother.

"Mom, seriously, that's not necessary. I'm 17 years old. I'm perfectly capable of staying by myself for the weekend." Seventeen going on two thousand. Too bad I couldn't mention that.

"I know," she sighed. "And it's not that I don't trust you. It's just that I worry. What if there's another earthquake?" She looked around my dismantled room. "I don't want you home alone in that case."

"Mom, I'll be fine. I wasn't even scared. Honestly."

"Hmm. Okay, maybe," she murmured. "And maybe is a maybe, not a yes."

I smiled. "Okay. Maybe."

"I don't think you should go to school today," she announced as the room shuddered once again with an aftershock. "It would make me more comfortable to have you at home. And besides, you have a mess to clean up."

I looked around. That was an understatement. It looked like a train had hit my room. And from somewhere amid the chaos, I could hear the muffled ring of my phone. I knew it was Gavin, calling to check on me, so I scrambled around trying to find it. My mom pulled it out from under my broken lamp and handed it to me.

"I'm going to get ready for work," she said. "Have a great day. I'll call you later."

I nodded as I answered my phone.

"Are you alright?" Gavin asked, not bothering to even say hello. I smiled at his obvious concern.

"Yes, I'm fine. My room is trashed though. How about you?"

"I'm fine. My room's fine. You know..." his voice turned suggestive and I could practically see him waggling his dark eyebrows. "If you need someplace to sleep, my bed's available."

I laughed. "Right. Your mom would love that."

"Minor hurdle," he replied with a grin.

I knew he was grinning. I could hear it. I absolutely loved his smile. It was the sexiest thing on earth. Thoughts of how we had spent so many afternoons in Cleopatra's palace in Alexandria invaded my thoughts and distracted me. I could still practically feel the taste of his lips and the feel of his rock-hard muscles beneath my fingers. This wasn't helping. I forced my thoughts away from the pleasurable ones with a sigh.

"Speaking of moms, mine doesn't want me to go to school today, so you don't need to come pick me up. I've got to stay here and clean up this mess."

As I spoke I looked around and groaned. What a disaster. My fingers itched to pick it up right now. The clean freak in me was about to emerge with a vengeance.

"Hmm. Staying home, huh? Need some help?" Gavin's husky voice was hopeful and oh-so-sexy and I felt myself waver. Then I thought the better of it.

"I'm thinking that if you came over, I wouldn't get anything done."

"Well, you would, but it wouldn't help your room," he conceded. "But I miss you. I need to see you today. Want to grab some dinner tonight?"

"Absolutely," I replied. "Just not that Italian place."

"Agreed," he replied. "No arguments there. I'll come by after school. I love you."

"I love you too."

"By the way… thanks for the late night text. What's up with that?"

I knew he would ask.

"I don't know. I just couldn't sleep and I wanted to be close to you."

"Hmm. Okay. Well, I love you more than life, too. Now get some work done and I'll see you soon."

I sighed as I hung up the phone. I loved everything about him. His face, his voice, his sweet soul. It was astounding that the millennia hadn't changed him a bit. I briefly wondered if it had changed me, as I stooped to pick up the clothes that had scattered from my drawers.

As I moved, my bloodstone swung away from me and clanged into my dresser. I clutched it and tucked it back into my nightgown. I focused very hard on trying to remember the detail surrounding it, but my memories of it were murky and I knew that was how the Moirae wanted it.

The bloodstone was powerful, so they didn't want me to be able to harness that power. Yet somehow, I had a sneaking suspicion that my necklace, the necklace in the legends, was tied to my bloodstone in some way. I could just feel it.

I stared at the pile of dripping glass heaped in the middle of my floor and sighed yet again. What a mess. I so wished that it was already cleaned up. I needed to make a research trip to the library and I didn't want to waste hours cleaning up earthquake debris.

Within the breadth of one second, before I had barely even finished my thought, the glass was gone. The wetness that had saturated my carpet was completely dry, not a spot, not a stain. I gasped.

How had I done that? I glanced around my room and saw the shattered pieces of glass in my wastebasket next to my desk. What the heck? I had briefly pictured my floor as the clean area that it had been- and all of a sudden, it became that way. Ho-ly crap.

My gifts. Harmonia's gifts. They were coming back to me.

I focused hard on the rest of my room, picturing my dresser upright and my clothes neatly folded within its drawers. It instantly became so. It didn't happen in front of me in a blur of motion, it was just...there. One moment it was a mess, the next moment it was clean, as though it had always been that way. I swallowed. What else could I do that I hadn't remembered yet? It was both an exciting and a petrifying thought.

I wished that the Moirae had allowed my memories to come fully back to me. I could remember bits and pieces of my life as a goddess, but nothing very cohesive or concrete. Just brief flashes. Gavin as Cadmus... his voice, his smile. It was the same. His touch on my back, his kiss on my neck. I could remember those things. I could remember scant flashes of life on Olympus, but no details. It was frustrating.

Regardless, I needed to put that out of my mind and focus on the present. I needed to learn more about the necklace of the legends... Harmonia's Necklace.

I grabbed some clothes and ducked into my bathroom, stopping short in front of the mirror in awe. My face had indeed transformed. It was subtle, not something you would be able to put your finger on. It was more like a vague radiance. My face had gotten thinner and more elegant, losing the baby fat that I had still been carrying in my cheeks. My vivid eyes remained the same. I turned from my reflection, yanking my hair into a ponytail before I grabbed my car keys.

I was at the library 10 minutes later.

As I walked through the hushed halls, I felt as though I was being watched. It was unnerving because every time I turned around, there was no one there. No one seemed bothered by the earthquake from this morning. I passed a few racks of books that had been disturbed, but library aides were busily re-shelving them. Apparently, there hadn't been any real damage.

I passed the coffee bar, inhaling the rich scent of roasted fresh coffee beans before I entered the main hall. I loved this library. It felt elegant and familiar with its dark wood panels and cozy lamps. I had been coming here since I was a kid. As I turned the corner, though, a hushed murmuring enveloped me... vague whispers. I whirled around, but there was no one there. And no one around me seemed as though they could hear it. I continued on to a tiny reading nook, trying to ignore the voices.

Dropping my stuff into a chair, I punched "Harmonia's Necklace" into the nearest resource computer. A plethora of book choices popped up and I scribbled them all down. I spent the next five minutes filling my arms with books on mythology and then settled myself into an overstuffed leather chair to pore through them.

There were conflicting stories. Some said that no descriptions of the necklace were available, while others said that it was a two-headed serpent. And while I couldn't conclusively rule that out, it didn't feel right. I didn't think it had been a snake.

I kept reading, filing each bit of information away as I read, but nothing was earth-shattering. It was all stuff that I already knew. My step-father had created a necklace to gain revenge on my mother for her infidelity. Unfortunately for me, he gave me the necklace, not my mother. So not fair. I was supposed to be cursed for all of eternity because of my mother's actions. What the books didn't contain though, was the fact that Zeus had contributed his own blood in order to make my necklace so powerful. The idea of how powerful it really was was alarming.

I fingered my bloodstone. With each breath I took, I was more and more convinced that somehow, the bloodstones *were* Harmonia's Necklace. The Fates must have somehow managed to use the one stone from my necklace to create more necklaces, one for each Keeper and one for each of the Fates. Hephaestus could have done that for them- he was the blacksmith to the gods. He could create anything which might be why they kept him chained to their door.

And realization fell on me like a ton of bricks. *Of course.* They kept Hephaestus near because they needed him. My necklace had been tied to me, which must have been the reason that they had chosen me to be a Keeper. They needed its power, but in order for them to access it, I still needed to have possession of it in some form. They needed me.

I remembered Lachesis' words when I was in Alexandria, right after I had lost my bloodstone. *The bloodstones were made from one stone. One. When one is lost, we all suffer…Our power as a whole should not be diminished because of the carelessness of one, should it?*

Oh my god. She admitted that the stones came from one stone. Their power was diminished because I had lost mine. And I was the key. I felt like I was going to hyperventilate. I sat hunched over trying to breathe… to make sense out of the craziness. I was a goddess. I had been cast into doomed mortal lives because I had been given a cursed necklace made from Zeus' blood. Life was not fair.

As I attempted to breathe, I caught a glimpse of movement from in front of me and I lifted my head. An ethereal woman was descending directly from the ceiling in front of me. She literally seemed to float down until she was standing one step in front of me. I looked around again. And yet again, no one seemed bothered. No one was staring or pointing or running and screaming. They couldn't see her. Interesting. I wasn't afraid. I could tell that she wasn't here to harm me. She had an air of serenity surrounding her.

She was dressed in white ancient Greek clothing, her blonde hair pulled loosely into a chignon. Her face was like porcelain, pale and perfect. She was so graceful that every movement seemed like dancing. I stared at her agape for just a moment longer before she beckoned to me with a slender finger.

"Come with me," she murmured softly.

As if I could do anything else. I trailed behind her as she led me to a secluded alcove.

She laid a leather bound book on the table in front of her. As she ran her fingers over the rich oiled surface, electricity jolted around the book. I startled.

"Who are you?" I asked breathlessly.

"They haven't returned all of your thoughts, Harmonia? That's terrible," she sympathized, her eyes warm.

"Who are you?" I asked again.

"I'm Alathea. The goddess of Truth. I'm not supposed to be here. If they find out...." Her voice trailed off before she steeled herself and spoke again. "I had to come because it pains me to have such lies and betrayal. You need this, Harmonia."

She gestured again toward the ancient book and tried to place it in my mind. It was definitely distinctive. Aged and tattered, it had clearly been around for awhile. Grape vines were embossed on the cover, twining around the spine and the back in an intricate design. But it didn't jog my memory.

"What is it?"

"The Map of Souls," she murmured. A tingling ran up and down my back. A Map of Souls?

"You're looking in the wrong place here," she continued, gesturing around at the library. "Your answers lie within this."

She patted the book and as she did, tiny leather fingers lapped up from the cover and grabbed at her skin. She paid them no mind and turned back to me. As she did, the fingers were absorbed back into the leather. It was unnerving.

"Your answers lie within," she repeated and handed it to me. I took it with reverence.

"Guard it with your life," she cautioned. "Tell no one that you have it and certainly not Alexi. I risked much to take it and bring it. Do not disappoint me, Harmonia. You and I are as sisters. You will remember that with time. When you do, you must help me."

"Help you?" I stared at her in puzzlement until I registered a strange, cold feeling settling around me. It felt like a thousand cold hands were rubbing my skin. A vague low moaning grew into a wail, something that the library patrons did not notice.

Out of the back wall, two shadowy figures emerged, wearing long black robes and hoods. They resembled grim reapers and my heart started skipping beats. They drifted quickly and with purpose across the main hall and within a minute, they had reached us, bringing with them a 20 degree temperature drop. I shivered.

"Yes, you will need to help me," Alathea said, holding her head proudly as they each grasped an arm. "Please."

The dark beings didn't say a word, but they didn't have to. Their mere presence was terrifying. They dragged Alathea back the same way they had come and disappeared into the wall. I stood in shock, clutching the book.

Now what?

My fingers trembled as they gripped the leather of the book and I felt the little fingers moving along the skin of my hand. My survival instructs kicked in and I did the only thing I could think of. I ran. I scrambled toward the reading nook and threw everything into my bag, flying as fast as I could out of the library and into the safety of my car. I sat behind my wheel, breathing heavily as I pondered what to do.

I had an overwhelming feeling that everyone around me was in danger while I was here. So, I turned the key and started driving. I didn't even know where I was going, but I needed to get far away from Pasadena while I figured it out. I drove straight out of the city through the congested traffic until I hit the highway.

And then I kept driving. I felt a strange pull luring me purposefully along the highway towards some unknown destination. I sighed and succumbed. I knew that it was best to just surrender and see what happened. I zoned out while the landscape flew past my car window. I didn't even turn the radio on as I lost myself in thought. I could practically feel things shifting- the air seemed strange and electric. I was being nudged toward something catalytic and it was terrifying, just as the unknown always was.

My phone vibrated against the passenger seat and glancing over, I saw Gavin's name on the screen. I was filled with trepidation. I wanted to talk to him, but he knew me inside and out. He would hear in my voice how upset I was and that would not work. He needed to remain in the dark. I let it go to voice mail. One minute later, he called again. I gulped and gripped the steering wheel. It was torturous not to pick it up, but I mustered up all of my available will power and once again let it slide into voice mail.

I looked into my rear view mirror and startled. Behind me, huge billowing dark clouds hovered ominously over Pasadena. They were much too large to be normal storm clouds and I felt the tension ratchet up into my neck. This. Was. Not. Good. The cloud wall grew larger by the moment, raging and bucking like a churning hurricane. No, this certainly wasn't good. That was not a normal act of nature.

There was a rest stop coming up on my right with a little café next to it, so I pulled off and parked. This was as good a place as any to contemplate what to do. The little restaurant's faded sign called to me, so I grabbed my purse, locked my car and crossed the dusty parking lot to the café.

As I opened the door, the bells over my head jingled, announcing my arrival. I quickly scanned the room for an empty booth and surprisingly encountered a familiar face. My heart lurched into my throat. There was no way this was a coincidence.

Jade was sitting in a booth at the back, her hands restlessly toying with her cell phone, an anxious look on her lovely face. I didn't even think as I made a bee-line for her, dropping unceremoniously down into the seat facing her. She looked up in surprise.

"Macy! You came. I'm not crazy," she murmured uncertainly.

"That's probably debatable," I replied wryly. "But no. You're not crazy. What made you think you were?"

"If I told you, you would definitely think that I am. So, let's just say that I felt like a drive."

"Or you could tell me the truth," I persisted. "Trust me, Jade. I am quite familiar with crazy."

She stared at me a moment, her eyebrows pulling into a knitted frown. I could tell that she desperately wanted to share it with me, but she just wasn't sure if she should. But our invisible bond was still there as strong as ever. Even if she couldn't see it, I knew she could feel it. She innately knew she could trust me and she finally sighed.

"I had a weird dream. A woman came to me and told me that I was more important than I knew, that everything was going to change and I was going to be at the heart of it. She said that I was not what I thought I was and that I should stay with you, that you would keep me safe."

"And so how did that bring you here?" I asked, trying my best to be patient.

"She told me to come here. She said to start driving and to go with my instincts, that she would lead me to you. And now here you are, just like she said."

I swallowed hard, trying to swallow my instant unease.

"I'm not crazy, am I?" she asked, her face developing a calm expression. "You're here, just like she said you would be."

"Yes, I'm here," I murmured. "You're not crazy. Did the woman tell you her name?"

"Yes. It was an odd name... Alathea."

Alathea had gone to Jade before she brought me the Map of Souls. And somehow, thinking of the two things in such rapid succession made me realize that they were connected. It just effortlessly clicked into place. Alathea wanted me to know who Jade was. And the Map of Souls could reveal that, so she had brought them both to me. The answer was within my grasp. I could barely breathe as I mumbled to Jade that I would be right back.

I stumbled out to the parking lot and dragged the book out of my bag. Leaning against my car, I opened the book, ignoring the fingers that grasped mine. The book contained intricate family trees that seemed alive. The names morphed and changed before my eyes as I turned each weathered page. My fingers numbly found Jade's name. I traced it backward through the millennia, my eyes widening as I saw who she had been in each life. And then I came to the first name. The beginning.

I could feel the pulse beating in my temple as I stared in apprehension at the letters on the page. The name was startling. Unexpected.

Aphrodite.

Jade was my mother.

Chapter Nine

*N*othing made sense.

Aphrodite was trapped in mortal form, too. So, that would mean that the rest of the gods probably were also. For what reason? The gravity of everything slammed into me and I had to force myself to concentrate. My goddess of a mother was sitting in a run-down, dingy diner in a ripped vinyl booth patiently waiting for me to explain to her who she was and why she was so special. A sudden feeling of déjà vu washed over me. In Alexandria, it was left to me to tell her that she was Cleopatra and that she was going to lose Egypt and die by her own hand. That was not a pleasant conversation.

And now here I was again. Same situation, different day. I was going to have to tell her that she was an Olympic goddess trapped in mortal form. How did one go about that conversation? I took a shaky breath. Carefully. The answer was *carefully*.

I tucked the Map of Souls back into my bag and trudged back toward the diner, each step bringing me one closer to the reckoning. My birthmark did not hurt. And suddenly, I was furious about the fact that it ever did. The Moirae had entrapped me, used me as a tool and had placed some sort of spell on me so that I experienced intense pain every time I did something they didn't like? That was not right and I briefly wondered how to go about getting it removed.

But I would have to ponder that later. As I reached for the door, I glanced once again toward Pasadena. The heavy black clouds were still rolling over the city. And I knew, without any doubt, that I needed to get to Gavin. My Cadmus. After I explained to Jade, he would be in danger. Which meant... maybe I should wait until I returned to tell her. I needed to somehow make sure that I kept Gavin safe. I suddenly felt so lost. Without Ahmose, I had no one to advise me. I was all alone and it was a horrible feeling.

I rushed back into the diner and slumped into the seat across from Jade. She watched me in anticipation, certain that I was going to change her life somehow. And I would. Just not right this second.

"Jade, can you trust me? I have something very important to tell you, but it is of utmost importance that I get back to Pasadena first. Can you trust me?" I asked her again.

She stared at me wide-eyed and nodded slowly. I noticed that her knuckles were white as she gripped her phone. Jade was my mother. It was a breathtaking revelation. I had been guiding her into making horrible decisions for herself for two millennia. That knowledge was killing me as I stared at her. The Moirae were truly sick. And I suddenly knew, with every ounce of my being that they were the enemy here. I needed to somehow contact the Keres. The old saying *the enemy to your enemy is your friend* suddenly made a lot of sense.

"Let's take my car. I don't think we should separate."

She nodded again, throwing some cash on the table and silently unfolding herself from the booth before she followed me to my car.

As we hurtled down the road toward the blackness ahead of us, Jade turned to me apprehensively.

"Is this about my DNA?" she whispered.

"What do you mean?" I asked hesitantly. How much did she know?

"My DNA," she sighed. "I'm a freak of nature and it's caused me nothing but problems since I was born."

She looked at me waiting for me to confirm it, but I just stared at her in puzzlement, before returning my eyes to the road.

"Um, I don't know what you're talking about."

She looked at me doubtfully.

"My DNA is weird. Because of my dad. He's a molecular physicist and after my sister died of a weird disease when she was a baby, he and my mother conceived me... in a Petri dish. He managed to manipulate my molecular structure to ensure that I wasn't born with the same hereditary illness. But in the process, he somehow altered my DNA so that I'm very... strange. You know that day at your pool?"

I nodded, knowing where this was going.

"You were right. My arms were scraped. But in the few seconds that it took you to reach me from the pool house, they healed themselves. I'm a freak. My dad has been working on trying to replicate the process for years. And that is why I live with my grandmother. He's afraid that if the scientific world hears of it, I'll be in danger. There are crazy people out there who would want to use me as a guinea pig. If they got a hold of me and recreated whatever anomaly that caused my DNA mutations, they could make impenetrable armed forces and crazy things like that. So, he hid me at my grandmother's."

I remembered the vision of Jade lying in a sterile hospital room, restrained to the bed and I stiffened. The Moirae wanted that outcome. But why? That had the potential to create world wars.

I shook my head. This was so much bigger than me or Jade. And I had a feeling that Annen could help us figure it out.

"Wow. The sky is so dark," Jade commented, staring ahead of us. "I've never seen it look like that before."

Because you've never seen pissed off gods before, I thought.

"It does look like all hell is going to break loose," I agreed aloud. "Could you do me a huge favor? Could you call Gavin for me? He tried to call me earlier and I couldn't pick up my phone."

She nodded and pulled out her phone. I watched her dial and then wait. She shook her head. "Voicemail."

"Okay. Will you just leave a message and ask him to call me?"

As she did, I suddenly remembered that there were two voicemails on my phone from him. I flipped my phone open and held it to my ear.

"Hi, beautiful. Hey, you're not going to believe this but Tara Wilson is here looking for you. She wants to apologize or something. So call me. I love you."

My heart froze. Tara was with Gavin? There was no way that she wanted to apologize. Something wasn't right here. With numb fingers, I pushed the button to listen to the second message.

This time Tara's voice filtered through the phone, but I knew in that instant who Tara really was. Was nothing what it seemed to be? I swallowed.

Tara was Eris, the goddess of strife and discord. My polar opposite. As Harmonia, I was the goddess of peace and contentment. Eris had been a thorn in my side for as long as I could remember. She could appear in any form that the wished and her normal purpose in life was to undermine me in any way that she could. And now she had Gavin. I listened to her icy voice with dread.

"Harmonia, I have Cadmus. The poor dear thinks he's in love with me. Can you believe that? Find me and don't dally. Bring your bloodstone and the Map of Souls."

The phone went dead and it was all I could do to not scream. My fingers turned white as I gripped the steering wheel and Jade stared at me in alarm.

"What is it? Macy, you're scaring me. What is going on?"

I took a deep breath and pulled off to the side of the road. Turning to face her, I started to speak and then closed my mouth. Where should I begin?

"Just say it," she said nervously, her hands twisting in her lap. She was wearing her amethyst ring and it glinted in the light. I sucked up my courage and just started talking.

"Jade, I have to tell you something and it is going to sound crazy, but I swear to you on everything holy that I am telling you the truth."

She nodded, her face very, very pale. She could feel the tension in the car, I could tell. How could she not? I could practically touch it with my hands.

"You are not what you think. And I'm not what you think. And that's what this is all about."

She raised an eyebrow.

"And? Are you going to tell me that you're a vampire or I'm a superhero or what?"

She laughed nervously, waiting to hear what craziness would come from my mouth. I didn't laugh with her. Instead, I pulled my bloodstone from around my neck and folded her fingers around it. Her head immediately was thrown back against the seat and I literally watched sparks fly from her hands as she gripped the stone. Her eyes were tightly shut, but I could see her eyes moving rapidly behind her eyelids as she followed the rapidly moving visions.

I knew what she was feeling. I had been there myself. And it wasn't fun. I felt guilty for thrusting it on her as I did, but there was no way I would have been able to explain so that she would believe me. She needed to simply see it for herself. I sat silently in my seat, waiting as patiently as I could. After three minutes or so, her eyes fluttered open and when she turned to look at me, her eyes were no longer the same.

They had turned the silvery gray color of an Olympic goddess.

I jumped from surprise, but tried hard to retain my composure. As it was, I still subconsciously scooted away from her towards my car door.

"What is it, Harmonia?" she asked curiously. I couldn't seem to make my tongue work, so I simply turned my rearview mirror in her direction. She peered into it and then sat back in her seat. "Oh, my. That won't do, will it?" she asked, looking at me again with her gleaming goddess eyes. I found myself thankful that minor goddesses didn't inherit those things. I would be unnerved every time I looked in a mirror.

"No," I agreed. "We can't let anyone see you until we get you some contacts or something."

She shook her head. "It won't matter. I can feel it. Something's coming. Nothing will be the same." She turned to me.

"Thank you," she whispered. "For awakening me. You did the right thing."

"You think?" I asked doubtfully. "I don't know what we are going to do. Did it restore all of your memories or...." I let my voice trail off as I stared at her pensively.

She shook her head. "No. But enough of them. I know who I am, who you are and where we came from. What I don't understand is why we are here...." She held up her arm and examined it as though she was looking at herself through new eyes. And I guess, in a sense, she was. It was always so strange to see things with fresh eyes once old memories had returned. I ought to know.

"We have to get to Gavin," I said. "This isn't his fault. None of it is. I cannot allow any harm to come to him and I don't know why they have him." I shuddered. "You don't know what they did to Ahmose."

Brief flashes of that torturous scene flew into my mind and I tried to shake them from my memory. This wasn't going to help. I tried to dampen the panicky feelings that were fluttering in my chest. I couldn't help him if I melted down.

"We need to find Annen. He works with the Keres and he'll know what to do. I can feel it."

"Annen works with the Keres?" she asked in surprise. "That is interesting news."

"Well, I doubt the Keres are the same as you are thinking..."

And as we continued the drive into the city, I continued to explain everything that I knew so far, including how Hephaestus was chained to the door in Zeus' palace. We were pulling into the city limits by the time I wrapped it up and the look on Jade's face was tantamount to hysteria.

"Calm yourself," I cautioned. "We can't accomplish anything if we are hysterical."

She nodded and I watched her chest heaving as she attempted to regain her control.

"This is surreal," she mumbled. "How can this be happening?"

"I don't know," I answered honestly. "But I feel the same way."

When we pulled into my driveway, my mother's car was parked there, gleaming mutely in the cloudy light. I turned off the ignition and glanced at Jade.

"Remember. You are Jade and I am Macy and that is that. Act normal. And put on your sunglasses." She quickly shoved her sunglasses onto her nose and we hurried into the house.

This time, when we entered, Hamlet went running away from us, diving under a kitchen chair. He laid there trembling, keeping a constant eye on Jade.

She turned to me in amazement and I just shrugged. Pets had crazily accurate senses. He knew something wasn't right. He was probably afraid of me, too, but since I still smelled the same, he overlooked it.

We continued on, bumping into my mother as we headed down the hall toward my bedroom. She was carrying an overnight bag.

She sighed in obvious relief. "Sweetie, I'm so glad you came home. Since it looks like a nasty storm is building, I'm going to head on out for my conference. I still haven't gotten a hold of your father, so I've decided that you can either come with me or you can stay here. Or you can probably go over to the twins' house. I'm sure their mother won't care. It's up to you."

"Um, I was actually just going to ask if Jade could stay here with me and keep me company. Her grandmother will be home if we need anything and we have a huge history final to study for." Lie.

But my mom didn't even notice in her rush. "I guess that's fine, honey. I trust you. Just remember the rules. Gavin can't stay past 10:00. Be the good girl that I know you are." She raised her eyebrows at me in warning and I smiled what I hoped was a reassuring smile.

"Mom, I promise. We're not going to do anything but study." And try to find our way to Mount Olympus.

She nodded. "Alright then. The hotel number is on the fridge, I have my cell phone and I left money on the counter for pizza or whatnot. I think you're all set."

She swooped in and gave me a hug and I clung to her for a minute. I didn't know what would happen and I felt suddenly sentimental. She pulled away and looked at me worriedly.

"Are you sure you're fine with staying alone?"

I nodded. "Completely. Have fun at your conference!"

She gave me another kiss on the cheek and then she was gone.

Jade and I rushed to my room where we dug out the Map of Souls and my bloodstone and sat on my bed. Jade fingered through the book while I clutched the pendant, silently willing Annen to us. He didn't appear. I murmured aloud and he still didn't appear. I sighed.

"I don't know what to do to get him to come," I admitted.

"He'll come," Jade assured me. "I can just feel it. And there's something else that I feel. I feel like we should leave. Do you feel that? It's like…. something is urging me to start moving."

And in that moment, I felt it too. I needed to move to my car. Something was pulling me.

"Well, there's only one thing to do," I murmured as I looped my bloodstone back around my neck. "We need to go."

We grabbed our purses and the book and practically ran to my car. Overhead, the sky looked angrier than ever and was rapidly turning as black as night. The wind had picked up, the trees whipping every which way. Anyone else would think just what my mother did, that it was a storm. But I knew otherwise.

I backed quickly out of the driveway and started driving in the direction that I felt the pull.

"Do you know where we're going?" Jade asked.

"No. You?"

She shook her head. "This is all so strange to me. Familiar and strange at once. I feel as though I should be able to do something, but I can't remember how."

I knew the feeling.

I blindly drove to the outskirts of town to a wooded hiking area. I looked around and stared nervously at Jade.

"This can't be good. We're isolated out here."

"That's probably the point," she pointed out.

"So not comforting," I grumbled as we got out.

There was no one here, but I suddenly felt the need to walk into the forest and as I did, my stomach tightened in anticipation. Whatever was waiting for us, I had a strong feeling that it would be game changing.

As we entered the labyrinth of trees, the branches almost completely blocked out the light and so it seemed that we were in a mossy, damp world. As we walked further in, I realized that my goddess senses had emerged even more. Here, in the quite solitude of this small forest, I could smell the rotting sticks, the wet earth and even the freshly cracked branches. The woodsy aromas flooded my nose in a way that they wouldn't have before. I could hear forest life scurrying, even tiny bugs. I could hear their tiny legs scraping as they walked along the underbrush. It was incredible.

We walked to a small clearing which was encircled by trees. Wildflowers bloomed around me and tall grass waved. And suddenly, here in the stillness, we were surrounded.

All around us, magnificent women were seated on massive horses. They were fierce and beautiful and intimidating. As one of the horses moved, I saw a folded wing at its side. These weren't normal horses. Each woman was riding a Pegasus. They were wearing scant clothing made from leather and a bow and arrow was strapped to each of their backs. Their hair was long and wild and they had bulging muscles in their arms. I suddenly simply knew who they were.

"The Amazon," I breathed.

Jade nodded as she stood back to back with me as we pivoted in a slow circle. There must be at least twelve of them which meant that we were greatly outnumbered. The Amazon were not known for their kindness. The fact that they were here at all was alarming. They didn't typically venture outside of their home. I looked at the warrior in front questioningly and I felt recognition stirring. I knew her.

"You require our assistance, sister," she said stiffly. Her name was Ortrera, an Amazon queen. And when she called me sister, it was the truth. Her father was Ares, also. She was my half-sister.

"We've been called here," she announced. "I believe it has to do with our father's imprisonment. You will need our assistance to release him."

"Why do you care?" I asked curiously. The Amazon did not concern themselves with matters of men. They were a very female oriented society. In fact, they scorned males. To them, men were inferior. At my question, she shrugged.

"He gave me life," Ortrera acknowledged. "He taught me the art of war. I cannot stand idly aside any longer and watch these atrocities against our own. It must stop."

"So, you know what is happening? You know what the Moirae have done?" I asked.

"Of course. Everyone knows it, but it would have been futile to intervene before. We do not shirk from war, sister, but it would not have been a wise battle. Now, though, we feel that the time is rapidly coming when action is required or we will all perish."

"I think you are right, Ortrera," I murmured. "Do you know where Ares is?"

"No, that I do not know," she admitted, hefting her heavy bow to the other side of her back. Her mare stood quietly and still, just as you would imagine a war horse would. Her white face was painted with blue paint. I was sure, if I examined all of the other horses, I would find them to be mares as well. The Amazon's distaste for males was far-reaching.

"Do you know where Eris is?" I asked hopefully, but again she shook her head.

"I had a vision, Harmonia, and I could clearly see a house, yet I know not who is in the house or the location."

"But we do."

We all turned to find Annen stepping through the circle of warriors with two other priests. The priest on the left had spoken. Annen stared at me pointedly, his black gaze glittering. As always, I shivered. He smiled his jagged, silent smile and they crossed the circle to join us in the middle.

"We know where they are keeping Ares, as well as a few other key pieces of information," the priest continued as they stopped at my side. "We will eagerly share it with you. But you must trust us."

Trust the Keres. It went against everything that I had been taught. But I knew without any doubt whatsoever that we had no other choice.

Chapter Ten

"You will need this," the priest said, thrusting a small glass globe into my hands.

"What is it?" I asked, examining it. The blown glass was delicately situated on an intricate bronze base. The inside was empty save for wispy white fog that billowed about as I rotated the globe.

"It has the power to take you wherever you need to go," he replied.

As I looked at it, Gavin's handsome face appeared in the empty glass sphere, smiling his breathtaking smile into mine. My heart instantly overflowed with love for him and fear for his safety dropped into my stomach like a rock. I had to get to him. If something happened to him, I would never forgive myself. The priest's voice interrupted my thoughts.

"Cadmus has appeared because that is where you would most like to be- with him. The compass can read your emotions, knowing where you would most like to be led. If you have the desire to go elsewhere, you simply have to hold it and picture the location in your mind."

"That is incredible," I murmured, turning it over in my hands. The priest shrugged.

"Not really. You're simply so accustomed to the mortal world that you have forgotten what ours is like."

"Yes, I have," I agreed. "And it is very frustrating. How can I recover all of my memories- the ones that the Moirae are still withholding?"

Pain shot through me, dropping me to a squirming mass on the ground, as fiery heat exploded into my hand and shot up my arm. I rolled, holding my palm in my hand as I tried to regain my composure. The pain was so unexpected that it took my breath away. I sat up, clutching my hand to my chest and glaring at Annen.

"You have an interpreter now," I scowled. "There is no need to mutilate me."

He simply smiled in return, his creepy, jagged smile and I looked away, focusing instead on reading the words seared into my palm.

They are already yours.

I looked at him quizzically. "They are already mine? And don't even think about burning me again." I stared at the first priest, the one who had been talking.

"What does he mean?"

He hesitated and then spoke. "Harmonia, he means that your memories are there for you to take. You have forgotten how we work, what we are."

"So, remind us," Jade interjected. "I am most curious, as well."

The priest nodded, studying us both.

"Kind ladies, you are able to do anything that you open your minds to do. If you want your memories, get them. Block any feelings of self-doubt or logic and simply open your mind. That is how everything is done in the Spiritlands. Focus on retrieving thoughts about your true home, the Spiritlands, and see what happens. Close your eyes. Picture your mind as a muscle, flexing and straining against reality. Now relax that muscle. Let it drop." His voice was soothing as he murmured and I lost myself in its sound as I concentrated on relaxing my mind.

He was right. The mind was like a muscle. I fixated on relaxing it, loosening it, letting it fall slack and getting farther from the constraints of reality. A feeling of familiar peace washed over me and in that moment, that one tranquil second, I was Harmonia. I became her completely, embracing her strength. I was home in a way that I had not been for centuries.

I opened my eyes and found Annen nodding. The priest to his side smiled.

"You are whole now, Harmonia. I can see it."

I nodded. "Yes. I feel exquisite." I turned to Jade. "And you, Aphrodite?"

"Yes," she murmured in a husky voice. "I too feel like myself again. Thank you, priest."

I scanned the edge of the forest with my enhanced eyesight. I could see everything, every minute movement. It was a delicious feeling. I lifted my hand and gestured at the tree tops. Instantly, they began to bend and move, the wind picking up and fluttering my hair around my shoulders. I lowered my hand and the wind became still. I could control the elements. Fascinating.

"Stop playing, Harmonia," Jade murmured, smiling a little. I couldn't help but smile back. It was so wonderful to be back to myself.

Ortrera nudged her horse forward and she spoke.

"Harmonia, we need to move. We do not want to be on the outer rim of the Spiritlands at night."

I nodded. No, we certainly did not. The Spiritlands contained every sort of mythical creature imaginable and so many of them thrived at night. She reached her hand down.

"Ride with me, sister."

I hesitated for only a brief moment as I stood next to her massive mare. The horse's feather soft wings flared out, enormous and magical, and I grasped my sister's hand, allowing her to pull me up. Tucking my legs under the Pegasus' wings, I settled in behind Ortrera, my arms wrapped around her muscular waist. With her every movement, I could feel her taut muscles flexing. Her physique was incredible.

Another Amazon warrior pulled Jade up with her and before I even knew it, the horses were arranging themselves in a V-like formation, with Ortrera at the lead.

"Harmonia," the priest called.

I twisted around to look at him.

"Yes?"

"Don't underestimate Eris," he instructed solemnly. "She has been your adversary for many, many years. She knows you well."

I nodded. I knew. An image of Pothinus the eunuch's flaccid face flashed into my head. Eris was quite skilled at assuming any form she wished and plaguing me mercilessly. As Pothinus, she had almost killed Hasani in Alexandria. And me. She had quite a lot to answer for. I was looking forward to demanding those answers.

"I know," I agreed. "And thank you for the compass."

All three priests nodded in unison as the Pegasus' moved forward. I felt the horse beneath me quiver as she lifted into the air, her strong wings pulsing as she carried us higher. We sailed upward until we were several hundred feet in the air, flying among the clouds.

I titled my face back and allowed the wind to rush over me.

"What a delicious feeling, Ortrera!" I shouted above the noise. "You're so fortunate to fly!"

She twisted around to give me an incredulous look.

"Harmonia, you are able to do whatever you wish. You don't require a Pegasus."

I thought on that as we continued through the night. We were seemingly so close to the stars that I could touch them with cold, shaking hands. The altitude made me chilly and I shivered as I gazed at the stars. I leaned closer to Ortrera to share her body heat. I felt her smirk, but ignored it. The Amazon never showed weakness of any sort. Ortrera wouldn't admit she was cold if her life depended on it.

We had flown for an hour before my fascination with flying dimmed and I began to chat about other things with my half-sister.

"What do you think will happen, Ortrera?" I asked hesitantly.

She shook her head.

"I have no way of knowing, sister. I wanted to take a trip to the old witches before I came to you to get their prophecy, but there was no time. We should stop on our way through. It could be helpful."

I thought on that for a second, of the old witches that lived in the cave on the edge of the Spiritlands. Their cloudy blue eyes were ageless and had always unnerved me with their sightless wisdom. It was said that they could see the future, that they breathed fear and ate pain. I had never doubted it.

"Perhaps, but I don't wish to delay reaching Cadmus. Every moment he is with Eris is dangerous."

Ortrera nodded in agreement and we fell back into comfortable silence for awhile. It amazed me how I had been apart from her for so long, yet we were instantly comfortable with each other upon reuniting. Others were intimidated by her, but I had always stood in awe of her independence and strength. She was an incredible woman.

"What do you think of our father?" I murmured against her neck so that she could hear me.

There was a pause.

"I think that all hell will break loose when we release him from bond," she nodded in affirmation. "He will possess a fury unlike that ever seen. The Fates will tremble and then eventually they will fall. But we must focus on one step at a time, sister. We must recover Ares and Cadmus before we think ahead."

"They have used me as their plaything, Ortrera," I muttered angrily. "I have unwittingly kept my own mother imprisoned for centuries. Do you know the things I have encouraged her to do... the pain that has been inflicted upon her at my counsel? It is atrocious. And they must pay."

That realization, the need for revenge, grew in my chest like a building wave. It was suddenly all I could think of as my thoughts were consumed by it. They had taken the last two thousand years from me. Over and over, I had lived lives of great sadness... all at their whim, for their entertainment. Once I managed to free my father and Cadmus, then locate the other Olympic gods, they would most certainly pay.

Calm yourself, Harmonia.

Aphrodite's voice resounded in my head as though she had murmured into my ear. I turned to find her staring at me pointedly, her silvery gaze tied to mine.

Put aside your thoughts for vengeance...for now. You cannot become consumed by it. It will accomplish nothing. Trust me, daughter, they will pay. None of this was your fault. You have nothing but love for me. I know that.

I nodded mutely, fascinated by the knowledge that like the priests, we could also communicate without speaking. Was there anything that we couldn't do? Was it truly as easy as simply believing something was possible... and then it simply was?

As the Pegasus descended in the sky, I stared below us at the vegetation beneath us. We were rapidly flying toward a bubbling spring leading up to a crashing waterfall. It was surrounded by beautiful, lush greenery. I concentrated and within a few seconds, the vivid green vines and leaves had all shriveled and died. I gasped. With my mind, I had killed it all. I quickly concentrated again, flexing the muscle of my mind, willing life to return. And suddenly, it was so. The greenery sprang back to life, the rich green hues spreading quickly throughout the vines until it was once again fresh and new.

I was astounded. The priests were right. Nothing was the same as it was for mortals. The trick was simply in opening my mind and using it. It was almost unfathomable.

The horses all landed lightly on their feet and stood still, barely even breathing hard as we dismounted. They were certainly as tough as their owners. As I approached the waterfall, I innately knew what we needed to do to enter the Spiritlands. Water was the key. You could only enter through water. I could feel the others falling into step behind me as I waded through the water of the spring and approached the waterfall. The water was crisp and clean and splattered onto my face as I stood still on the slippery, mossy rocks.

Taking a deep breath, I stepped through the waterfall. Instead of stepping straight into a wall of stone as one might have expected, the stone faded away and I emerged on the other side in the Spiritlands. I stood in a stream with the waterfall at my back now, splattering against my shoulder blades in fat droplets. But on this side, instead of water it was made from nectar. I bent slightly and scooped my cupped hand in the icy sweetness, bringing it to my mouth to drink.

The nectar of the gods. The life force that kept us immortal. I felt it running down my chin, dripping onto my body but I didn't care. I simply drank more of the wonderfully delicious liquid. There had never been anything like it in the history of the world. I glanced down and saw the blood stains running down my shirt and grimaced.

As the others appeared behind me, I concentrated on my clothing. I pictured myself standing in Harmonia's traditional Greek clothing, a short, airy white shift that floated around my thighs like gossamer. It was corded around my ribcage in the empirical fashion. And of course, my bloodstone lay in its normal place against my chest. My jeans and bloody shirt were gone. One more step into the transformation of Harmonia.

I turned and found Jade similarly attired as Aphrodite. The Amazons looked on in approval as Jade knelt at the edge of the stream and drank from the nectar, as well.

"It is good to have you back," Ortrera observed. "I take comfort in it, sister. We will set things right. Come now, though. As I mentioned, we do not want to be out here once night falls."

I nodded and we once again mounted the horses. I shoved my long shift up around my thighs so that I could ride astride. Not ladylike, but it would have to do. The Pegasus' once again fell into formation and we began our trek through the dangerous outer rim of the Spiritlands.

Before we had even traveled five minutes, a raven with sparkling ruby eyes landed on my shoulder. I should have been startled, but my tolerance for all things strange had been appropriately raised once we had crossed the boundaries of my home. Instead of shirking away, I stared into its scary eyes without flinching.

"Dear Harmonia, your return is greatly anticipated," it croaked with its sharp beak. "It is time to fulfill the prophecy… to restore harmony and peace to Olympus."

I stared at the bird.

"What do you mean 'the prophecy'?" I asked curiously. "I have not heard of such a thing."

"Of course you have not," it sounded slightly indignant. "The prophecy came to be after you left. But you are the one. The one who will save us all."

I felt my heart flutter a little. I was the one to save them all? Nothing like a little pressure. I grimaced and turned to Jade.

"Did you know of this?"

She shook her head. "No. But I am not surprised. It is in your very nature to bring peace. Why wouldn't it be you? Besides, it was your necklace they took in the first place. It is only right that you will rectify it."

For the first time since recovering my memories as a goddess, I felt apprehensive. I was a minor goddess. How in the world was I going to save all of the Olympic gods? I wasn't sure I was capable. In fact, with the magnitude of that challenge staring me in the face, I felt pretty insignificant.

The raven fluttered off of my shoulder and flew away with a shriek. I watched it fly into the distance and disappear before I returned my gaze to the horizon.

The air here smelled like a heavily scented night garden. Freesia, moonflowers and primrose hung in the night like a curtain. I inhaled it, drawing in the fragrance and enjoying the taste in my mouth. I could taste the peace around me and I wondered how long that would last. The night was so dark, so velvety that I felt as if it was tangible, as if I could breathe it in, as well. I felt it clinging to my skin and caressing my body like unseen hands.

The landscape around me was beautiful. Night-blooming flowers were everywhere as the moon hung brightly above us. It was larger than I had ever seen it in the mortal world, huge and yellowy-red. Sailors in the mortal world called it a blood moon. Much like everything else around me, it was beautiful and larger than life.

The horses nickered softly to each other as they walked through the knee-high waving wild-grass. They were nervous. I could feel it suddenly, a palpable force in the air around us. Something was with us. The horses knew it too. I scanned the darkness, but even with my enhanced vision, I could see nothing. My gaze flew to Aphrodite's face.

"No," she sighed. "I see nothing."

Goosebumps formed on my arms and the hair on the nape of my neck raised in anticipation. Something was wrong. We were not alone.

Suddenly, a blackness so absolute that it almost blocked the light of the moon, appeared in front of us. Ortrera's horse reared up on its hind legs and I clung to Ortrera's back as she soothed her terrified mare. The horse quickly regained composure and stood at attention, the occasional flick of her ear the only sign of her distress. She was well trained.

The darkness became more and more visible, until it formed into the shape of a large black dog, then split into three... then morphed into three women. The witches. Hecate, the goddess of witchcraft, plus Circes and Medea. They lived in a cave on the outskirts of the Spiritlands, a cave which contained a direct connection to the Underworld.

They stood in front of us now, two of them dressed in long sweeping gowns of gray and black and straggly hair. They appeared as old, stooped women, their faces etched with wrinkles, their eyes cloudy and sightless. Yet they still followed our movement with uncanny precision. As always, they unnerved me. Hecate, however, appeared as a beautiful young woman. Her crimson gown was tight in the bodice and her full breasts spilled over the top. Her plump red lips parted, then spoke.

"Harmonia... Aphrodite," she murmured. "You did not trouble yourselves to stop as you passed. That was a mistake. We know what you need."

I hesitated.

"What do we need, witch?" I asked.

She tossed a tiny bundle to me, a little bag tied with string. I caught it easily and examined it. It had a putrid odor rising from it and I didn't even want to think about what it might be.

"What is this?" I questioned. "And why do we need it?"

"You will see," Circes muttered. "You will soon see. Do not forget us when you have finally reached Olympus. You will need us two more times before this battle is finished. And then we will expect reward."

"What kind of reward?" Aphrodite asked suspiciously.

"The kind that we deserve," Medea answered mysteriously. "We can discuss terms later. Just remember, you will need us again. And you will not win unless you use us."

And they were gone. As quickly as their darkness had surrounded us, it just as quickly lifted. The moon shone brightly again, beautifully lit against the blackness of night. I felt a renewed sense of urgency to reach Gavin. My Cadmus. It built slowly in the base of my stomach and grew until it filled my whole body, my entire heart.

"We must hurry," I murmured. "Time is short. I can feel it."

Ortrera urged her horse faster and we took off like lightening into the sky.

Within an hour, I could see a small limestone house below us. Light flooded from the windows, falling onto the waving grass outside and somehow, I innately knew that I would find Eris inside. This was her home. The horses descended from the sky, the roar of their moving wings softening as we lowered to the ground.

I slid to the ground and waited for everyone else to dismount. I could feel an invisible pull tying me to the house. Gavin was inside as well. I knew it with every cell in my body. I needed to reach him. Now.

I scrambled to the wide marble porch and peeked into the windows of the door. Eris was inside, lounging on a long plush couch. She had shed the orange tan and fake boobs that she had employed as Tara and was instead languishing in her true form. Black hair was coiled on top of her head and her pale blue eyes scanned the room and found my gaze as she sensed my presence. She smiled a satisfied, arrogant smile.

"Cadmus," she called

Gavin appeared from the doorway of another room, bare-chested and beautiful. My breath froze in my throat and I rattled the door to enter. It was locked. I stared in horror as Gavin crossed the room and bent to lock Eris in a passionate embrace. I couldn't breathe as he kissed her softly then deepened the kiss as her hands splayed across his bare back. This couldn't be happening. He was mine. I saw the muscles ripple in his back as he pulled her even closer and my heart broke. It was most certainly happening. I was watching it.

Over the shoulder of my soul mate, Eris gazed at me with a vicious, satisfied hate. I returned her stare proudly, but my heart was broken. How had she managed to take my very reason for life….the one thing that I had loved throughout the millennia?

Chapter Eleven

*A*phrodite laid a calming hand on my shoulder.

"Harmonia, Eris has done something to him. He would not abandon you for her willingly."

And I knew that, but I couldn't help but wonder how he had allowed it to happen at all? We were soul mates. Bound through time with a love stronger than steel. He was mine. And I was his. Unquestionably. Forever. Yet here we were. He was half-dressed and embracing my sworn enemy.

I heard footsteps falling on the stone inside the door and I steeled myself. The door was opened and I was suddenly facing him. Cadmus stared at me, no more than a foot in front of me. I desperately wanted to launch myself into his strong arms, to inhale the scent of his skin, but the look on his face stopped me in my tracks.

He didn't know me.

"Can I help you?" he asked politely, with the vague nicety of a stranger. I tried not to hyperventilate and recognized with sick humor that controlling emotions didn't get easier when you were a goddess. As I stood frozen, Jade came to my rescue, stepping up to my side.

"Hello," Jade answered, sticking out her slender arm. The gold bracelets on her wrist glinted in the light and caught my eye. I focused on them. Anything to avoid seeing the blankness on Cadmus' face. She continued in a soothing, sweet voice.

"I'm Aphrodite. I don't know if we've met."

Cadmus took her hand and raised it to his lips, briefly kissing her hand in a polite Olympic way. He shook his head.

"No, we haven't had the pleasure. I'm Cadmus. And I am very happy to meet you."

"We've come to speak with Eris," Jade continued. "Might we come in?"

He nodded and pushed the door open wider. As we walked past him, I caught a whiff of his distinctive scent and my eyes filled with tears. I wanted him back. Right now. He was mine and this wasn't fair.

My inner turmoil was in such a rage that the torch that I had just walked past exploded into flame. I jumped away from it, breathing hard. I had forgotten that could happen. It was imperative to control my emotions or accidents might result. I focused hard on controlling my breathing, on slowing it down to a normal pace as we drew to a stop in front of Eris.

She lounged on her couch, smiling a wide Cheshire cat smile. I wanted to throw up. Or attack her. Instead, I squared my shoulders and stared at her coolly.

"What have you done, Eris?" I asked.

"I have no idea what you mean, Harmonia," she replied.

She looked past me to Cadmus.

"Cadmus, darling. Please come sit with me. I have the need to feel you near."

She patted the seat next to her and I shuddered as he obligingly walked to her and sat. He would never, ever do that if she hadn't enchanted him somehow. He wasn't an obedient pet, yet she was treating him like a lap dog. And he was allowing it.

"What have you done?" I asked again through clenched teeth.

I could hardly stand to watch as she ran her fingers lightly over Cadmus' toned arms, trailing lightly down his chest and resting familiarly on the top of his thigh. Instead of ripping her hand off, I steeled myself again and met her gaze.

"And again, I have no idea what you mean," she answered pleasantly. "Is it so far-fetched to imagine that Cadmus just acquired better taste and prefers me to you?"

I gritted my teeth. "He doesn't even know who I am. You've done something, you wretched snake."

At the venom in my voice, Cadmus raised his gaze to mine, startled.

"Is there a problem?" he asked hesitantly.

"Yes," I answered, unable to help myself. "You are mine. We've been together for thousands of years. You don't belong here."

He laughed his rich, husky laugh and I realized that he thought I was joking.

"I think I would remember that, would I not?" he asked, with his chocolate eyes twinkling. A part of me died as I stared at him, seeing no familiarity whatsoever in his gaze. I shook my head weakly.

"You would think," I muttered.

He spoke again.

"Sweet Eris, we should invite your friends in for the night. The Chimeras will be out soon. You wouldn't want them to get waylaid by one."

Eris shook her head slowly, a small smile curling the corner of her lip. "No, that would indeed be tragic, dear Cadmus."

I couldn't help but think of the Chimera, a wretched species of beast. Part lion, part goat and part snake. It had two heads... one lion, one goat. Its tail was a snake and both ends could breathe fire. It flew in the blackness of night with the wings of a dragon and it wailed a horrific shrieking wail that could literally curl your toes. Thank god they were rare. But still. They were out there somewhere in the night, which meant that we shouldn't be if we could help it. I hated to take shelter here, but at the same time, it would give me more time with Cadmus.

I nodded. "Thank you, dear friend," I emphasized the last word. "We would be ever so grateful for your shelter." I almost choked on the words but somehow managed to spit them out.

Cadmus grinned. "Wonderful. Any friend of Eris' is a friend of mine. I will see to your rooms."

He pushed off of the couch and strode from the room with his familiar loping walk. I watched his broad shoulders disappear through the doorway before I turned to Eris once more.

"What did you do?" I hissed.

"As if I would tell you," she purred. Her satisfaction was blatantly obvious and I worked to temper my own reactions. There was no need to make her rejoice even more in my despair. I felt Ortrera step forward from behind me.

"My warriors will be outside guarding our horses," she murmured to me. "I shall stay inside with you."

I nodded mutely while Cadmus reentered. His face was so beautiful, his dark hair curling slightly around the nape of his neck. I needed to feel him under my fingers, kiss his soft lips. But I couldn't. Yet. I swallowed hard.

"Your rooms are ready," he announced. "If you would come with me, I'll show you the way."

"Don't be gone long, Cadmus dear," Eris sang. "I shall need you again shortly."

He nodded, smiling in her direction while I cringed. Need him for what? I tried not to think about it as I followed my soul mate down the long hall to the bedchambers.

He opened one heavy door. "This will be yours," he said to Ortrera. "Aphrodite, you will be across the hall. And Harmonia, you will be here."

He opened the door to my room and I walked swiftly past him into the room. He trailed behind me. "I think you will find everything you need," he said quietly. "If you need something else, just let one of us know." He turned to walk out.

"Cadmus," I began. And he turned.

"Yes?" His dimples appeared as he smiled and my heart took off like thunder. I focused on calming down for a moment before answering.

"Um. I would like to bathe before bed. Could you point me into the direction of a bath?" I shot a weak smile in his direction, unable to do or say anything else. It wasn't the time. I could feel it.

"Of course. I'm sure you are tired," he smiled sympathetically. "The bath is the door to your right. Make yourself at home."

He turned to leave and this time I let him. I sank into the silken bedclothes adorning the bed and sobbed with my face pressed into a pillow to muffle the noise. I had been so worried about his safety—so scared that Eris would harm him. I had never, in a thousand years, imagined that she would take him from me. She had taken Derek to toy with me. And that had been child's play for her. Derek had been so easy for her to win over. But this... to steal a soul mate. She had to have had help. Very powerful help. But what?

I felt a cool hand on my back and I opened a puffy eye, watching Jade slide onto the bed next to me. Her expression was empathetic as she curled up behind me, pulling me up next to her as she stroked the hair from my brow.

"Shh," she soothed. "I know it is hard now, sweetling. But this isn't forever. We will get to the bottom of this and Cadmus will once again be yours."

I cried even harder as she murmured the sweet words. I knew they were true, but the knowledge that he was with Eris at this very moment doing god only knows what... it was too difficult to bear. I cried silently for a while longer while Jade stroked my back.

My eyes were burning and red by the time I was finished. I sat up and wiped at them impatiently.

"I'm sorry, Aphrodite," I muttered. "I know you are right. I just feel so alone without him."

"You aren't alone," she assured me. "I am here. Ortrera and her warriors are here. And we will fix this atrocity. All of it."

I turned to her and stared into her silver eyes. And nodded. She was right. We would fix it. No matter what it took. Cadmus was most certainly mine.

"I think I will take a bath," I sighed. "I wonder if it is safe?"

Aphrodite nodded slowly. "I doubt she will attempt anything in front of Cadmus. But just in case, Ortrera and I will be on guard. Go and relax in the bath. I will take one after you."

I nodded and slipped from the room, determined to soak my troubles away.

I ran a steaming bubble bath and willed it to be scented with honeysuckle. Instantly, of course, it was. The soothing scent rose from the hot bath and filled the bath chamber. I inhaled it as I closed my eyes and breathed long, deep breaths. Through the walls of the house, I could hear Eris and Cadmus laughing together; familiar and affectionate. It made me want to scratch her eyes out. I gritted my teeth and tried to tune it out.

Twisting my hair into a pile on my head, I let my white sheath fall to the floor around my ankles and I stepped into the sunken tub, wearing only my bloodstone. There was no way I was taking it off. Not in this house. Slipping under the water until the bubbles rose to my chin, I closed my eyes, relishing the way the hot water soothed away my tension and aches. Too bad it couldn't reach my heart. Even still, I rested quietly until the slightest of noises caused my eyes to flutter open quite some time later.

I stared into Cadmus' startled face. In the light of the candles lining the wall, his face was bronzed and oh-so-handsome. His bare chest glistened in the light and I could see the shallow breaths that he was taking as his ribs rose and fell. He was so close I could reach out and touch him. I could barely stand it.

"I'm so sorry," he uttered quickly, backing toward the door. "I didn't know you were still in here."

"Don't go," I cried, lunging up out of the water.

Water sloshed out of the tub and I stood completely naked in the middle of it with water streaking down my body in rivulets. I was satisfied to see that his gaze quickly slid down my body before he tore his beautiful dark eyes back up to my face.

"I'm sorry," he murmured again. "My apologies, truly."

"You have nothing to be sorry for," I answered quietly. "This is your home, is it not?"

He nodded silently, clearly unsure what I was wanting from him. I wanted *him*, damn it. Only him. Right now. I was tired of Eris' games.

"Could you hand me that towel, Cadmus?" I asked quietly, still very aware of my naked status. My breasts were feeling the effects of the cold air and they tilted upward as the skin around my nipples tightened. Goosebumps formed on my legs and I wished them away. I wanted to look perfect in the light of the candles... for him. For my soul mate. I needed him to know who I was.

He visibly swallowed and leaned to grab the towel lying near me, quickly handing it to me. I noticed that his fingers were shaking and he tried very hard to keep his eyes averted. Bless him, the sweet soul. He was even a gentleman when he couldn't remember who he was. But that wouldn't do. Not tonight.

I propped my leg on the side of the bath and leaned over to rub it dry, hoping against hope that I looked sexy as I did it. I had never been what you could call a Siren. That was more up Aphrodite's alley. But I knew that I was beautiful. It had never mattered before but I was counting on that fact right now. And I knew that Cadmus found me beautiful. He had told me a million times before. Surely he could feel our connection. Surely.

My long hair had fallen around my shoulders and I chanced a glance through the dark strands at his face. He was staring at me, standing ever-so-still a few paces away. He looked poised for flight.

"I shouldn't be here," he murmured nervously.

"But you are," I answered. "Do you wonder why?"

I stepped from the tub, allowing the towel to fall to the floor. I approached him, wearing only my bloodstone and a smile. Nervously, I stopped in front of him.

"I have to tell you something," I murmured as I stepped one step closer. I was now two inches in front of him. I could practically feel his breath on my face and I inhaled it, mesmerized by even that familiar smell. I knew every bit of him, from the feel of his hair to the touch of his fingers.

"What is it?" he asked. "I was supposed to return immediately to Eris. She will wonder where I am."

"Yet you are still here with me," I pointed out. "Do you wonder why that is?"

"Because there is a naked goddess standing in front of me?" he quipped. "I'm a man, not a monk."

"True," I conceded. "But you are a gentleman if ever there was one. You are only still here because you feel it too." I trailed my hands up his bare chest, marveling in the spark that I felt as I moved along his skin.

"What do I feel?" he whispered, his lips just mere inches from mine.

"You feel *me*. I know it," I insisted. "You know me, Cadmus. I've always been yours. I need you to remember. Please."

He took a step back, his face puzzled and confused.

"I don't know you," he answered. "I'm sorry. You must have me mistaken for someone else."

I shook my head. "No. I don't. You know me and I know you. Better than anyone has ever known someone else."

He stopped, but didn't come closer to me. So I remedied that by taking another step toward him.

"Don't," he whispered.

"Don't what?" I answered softly, running my hands up his chest and curling around his neck. "Don't do this?"

I pulled his head down to my waiting lips. His soft mouth enveloped my own, igniting a passion in me immediately. A fiery passion that only he could awaken because I was made for him. I sighed into his mouth and it startled him into moving.

He backed up once more.

"I'm sorry," he stuttered. "I can't. I don't know what I was thinking... I..." He turned to go, but I yanked my bloodstone over my head and shoved it into his hands before he could take one more step.

"You were thinking this," I answered.

He dropped heavily to his knees on the bathroom floor in front of me, his head bowed and his hands formed into fists on the floor. I knew he was being assaulted with every memory he had ever had, flitting in and out of his head in rapid fire. It was an alarming and confusing feeling. I knew- I had been there myself time and time again. The magic of the bloodstone was powerful and I knew it wasn't failing me now.

It lasted for several agonizing minutes. He kept his head bowed and remained still and unmoving. The only sign of his distress were his white knuckles grasping my bloodstone.

I waited patiently, wondering the entire time if it would be enough. *Please, please god... let him remember me,* I prayed. The irony of a goddess praying was not lost on me, but it didn't stop me from doing it. The honeysuckle air between us was charged and I breathed in short pants as I waited.

A few minutes later, I was rewarded.

Cadmus raised his head, his dark, tortured brown eyes staring into mine.

"Harmonia."

One small word, but he conveyed a million things in those four tiny syllables. He knew me.

He rose to his feet and turned to me, holding out my bloodstone for me to reclaim.

I bypassed it and flew into his waiting arms, burying my head into his chest as he pulled me close.

"Cadmus, thank god. Thank god. I thought I had lost you."

"I'm always yours, Harmonia," he murmured into my hair. "Even when I don't remember it."

He wrapped his arms around me tightly and dipped his head to once again to press his lips to mine. When he ended the kiss a moment later, I stared up him. I could feel the wetness forming in my eyes and I blinked hard.

"Don't ever leave me again, Cadmus. Please."

He smiled his gentle smile again. "Never. I promise."

Chapter Twelve

When we emerged from the bath chamber twenty minutes later, the house was still and quiet. There wasn't a sound…not a creak, not a laugh. The hallway was eerily empty, every door along the wall closed tight. My startled eyes flew to meet Cadmus'. Something was wrong. Again.

Cadmus reached back and grasped my hand tightly within his and I trailed behind him as we crept down the hallway. I peeked into Aphrodite's guest room and found her bed to be empty and unused. I gulped. Two steps later, I peered into Ortrera's room. She was sleeping soundly, lying perfectly still. I rushed to her side and shook her arm, attempting to wake her.

It was no use. She refused to stir. And something about the limp way she was lying gave me pause. Her long tangled hair was spread around her, her eyelashes rested gently upon her cheeks, her hands clasped at her chest. She looked dead. All she needed was a lily in her hands to complete the look. I looked anxiously up at Cadmus.

"This isn't right. She's not asleep, is she?"

He shook his head solemnly as he also attempted to rouse the Amazon queen.

"It doesn't look like it. Eris is very wily. It is hard telling what she has done."

We combed through the rest of the house quickly, finding Eris and Aphrodite gone. They had simply disappeared. I burst onto the porch to find the Amazon warriors inside a ring of fire. I assumed it was to ward off the Chimeras as they slept. But not even one warrior was awake to stand watch… something I knew was unheard of for them. They were nothing if not prepared and vigilant. As I moved toward them, I was already afraid that they were in the strange comatose state as well.

My fears were confirmed within a few minutes as we tried without success to wake them. How in the world had Eris managed this? She had somehow taken down thirteen fierce Amazon warriors. How, how, how? I wracked my brain, but came up empty-handed.

I turned to Cadmus.

"What do you think?" I whispered, reaching for his hand again. He grasped it, stroking my hand gently with his thumb as he thought. It was the most beautiful feeling in the world. Our hands fit together perfectly, as if they were created to do just that.

"It's clearly some sort of spell," he mused. "But what? And more importantly, how can we break it?"

As I absently sifted through my knowledge of spells and potions, I remembered the vile little bag that the witches had given us. I took off for the house like a shot, leaving Cadmus to stare after me in bewilderment. I felt him behind me within a few seconds as I bolted toward my guest room.

The tiny burlap sack was lying on my bed, right where I had left it. The top was cinched closed with twine and the closer I got to it, the more pungent the smell became. I wrinkled my nose as I picked it up.

"This is something important," I muttered. "The witches gave it to us earlier tonight and said that we would need it. Actually, they said that we would need them three times before this is over."

Cadmus leaned closer to stare at it.

"What is it?" he asked curiously. "It smells like death."

"I know. I'm afraid to know what it is."

Contrary to my words, I pulled on the string that held the bag closed. I didn't have the luxury of being squeamish. I had to open it. The bag fell open on the bed. I could only describe the contents as squirming, moving slime. It wasn't alive, but it was certainly churning and moving. Deep crimson red, it glimmered with a strange sparkle. In the middle, lay a silver dropper. On its body, the words *Resurrection, 2 drops* were inscribed. And as Cadmus had so accurately pointed out, it smelled like death.

But clearly, it was meant for us now.

I squared my shoulders, snatched it up and headed for Ortrera. She was still peacefully resting, oblivious to everything. I carefully measured two drops of the vile concoction into the dropper and gently put them into her mouth. Pushing her chin closed around the liquid, I waited.

Nothing.

And then she screamed, lurching up in bed and screeching at the top of her lungs. I clapped my hands over my ears and Cadmus cringed. The sound was deafening.

After a moment, she stopped and looked at me in bewilderment.

"What happened? Why am I screaming?"

"I have no idea," I answered. "Eris enchanted you somehow. Did you eat something or…"

"Of course not," Ortrera answered, sounding indignant. "I would never eat something here for just that reason."

"Then I have no idea how she managed," I replied. "But that's neither here nor there. Right now, we need to revive your warriors."

Rushing outdoors, I knelt next to each inert warrior and carefully administered the potion. Each woman reacted in the same way as Ortrera, by lurching upward with a screech. It was unsettling, to say the least. After I was finished and the women had come to their senses, I stared at Cadmus and the Amazon queen.

"Now what? Eris has taken Aphrodite. And we don't know where. I almost think that she took Cadmus as a distraction. She knew that I would be distracted with trying to get Cadmus to remember me… and her true purpose was to separate me from Aphrodite. I'm such a fool- I played right into her hands. It was never about Cadmus at all."

"Sister, don't distress. The only ones that Eris can possibly be working for are the Fates," Ortrera reminded me. "We will head for them and I am certain we will find her."

I nodded, staring absently into Cadmus' dark eyes. It was probably a trap. But there wasn't anything we could do but walk right into it.

Ortrera turned to her warriors.

"Mount up! We ride now!"

The women lumbered to their feet, slinging their quivers and bows back onto their backs and I was once again taken aback by their fierceness. They were not afraid of anything, come what may. I wished I could be the same. A quote that I had heard once suddenly rang in my ears and it had never seemed truer to me. *Courage is not being fearless- it is created by overcoming your fears*. That was certainly true in my case and I definitely had a lot of fears to overcome.

I climbed behind Ortrera as another warrior rode with Cadmus. The horses fell into their flight formation and we again took off into the sky like lightening. I held the compass firmly in my hands and fervently pictured Aphrodite. Peering into the globe, I saw nothing but white mist. The compass glowed like a night light in the darkness, but nothing appeared.

It seemed that we needed an exact place to focus on for the compass to lead us to it. I thought of visions of Zeus' palace and Olympus but still Aphrodite didn't appear. Curious.

I let the compass drop into my lap. Leaning my face against Ortrera's strong, leather-clad back, I closed my eyes, determined to rest for just a bit before we arrived at the Moirae's doorstep.

Sleep, my love. We're together again and I will never let you go.

Cadmus' deep, husky voice resounded in my mind and my eyes popped open to stare into his. He winked and smiled and warmth flooded through me. Whatever happened, it would happen with my soul mate at my side. I couldn't ask for more than that at this point. I closed my eyes and let the darkness overtake me. I was even more exhausted than I realized.

We had only flown for maybe fifteen minutes more before I heard Cadmus call to Ortrera.

"Let's stop. Harmonia can't even stay awake. Besides, we don't want to bring a fight in the dark. Let us stop and regroup and plan our strategy during the daylight hours."

Ortrera nodded and we began our descent to the ground. The Pegasus landed so smoothly that I almost didn't realize when the flying ended and the walking began. The night was so dark that I almost couldn't see. Before I even knew it, Cadmus had slid from his horse and was pulling me from mine, into the safety and warmth of his arms. I melted into him, enjoying the contact. I was disappointed when he pulled away a minute later. But he kept his hand clasped with mine as we assembled into a circular camping area.

One of Ortrera's warriors lit a fire in a circle around us as we conjured up bedding and pillows for sleep. Ortrera insisted that Cadmus and I remain in the middle of the circle, protected by her warriors. Cadmus rolled his eyes a little toward me, but then shrugged his shoulders. He knew it was no use to argue with the Amazons. They took their roles as warriors very, very seriously. Luckily, Cadmus was very secure in his manhood and didn't seem fazed by the protection of women. He seemed more amused than anything. That was something else I loved about him. He rolled with the punches.

I studied him as he strode across the circle toward me. The light from the fire reflected on his lean, muscular body, giving his olive skin an even more golden hue. Strange, but in Pasadena, I hadn't considered him to be built like a warrior. Clothed in modern clothing, he hadn't seemed the part at all. But here in the Spiritlands, with a low-slung wrap around his waist and his chest bare but for the diagonal leather strap of his flask, he seemed once again like the amazing warrior that I knew he was. He was at home here.

I watched as he withdrew his metal flask from the holster at his hip and then knelt by the fire, holding the flask over the flame. The orange glow lapped at his beautiful face and I sighed as I lay on my blankets. I wanted him here with me. I wanted to feel his hand within mine and absorb his strength.

As if he read my mind, he glanced at me and after wrapping his flask in a cloth, he rose and strode purposely toward me. Sitting cross-legged next to me, he handed me the wrapped metal bottle.

"Here, my sweet. I heated some nectar for you. It should warm you up. Drink it. Tomorrow might very well be long. You will need your strength."

I smiled at him gently, unable to resist his dimpled grin. I took the flask and sipped at it. He was right. The warmed nectar was wonderful. I felt the warmth slide down into my belly and it warmed my whole body. I hadn't even realized that I was cold until he had remedied the situation.

He wrapped a strong arm around my shoulders, pulling me close. I closed my eyes as we nestled into the blankets, pretending just for a second, that we were normal mortals. Normal mortals, however, would not be staring at the swirling sky of the Spiritlands.

As I stared upward at the stars, I couldn't help but marvel at the beauty surrounding me. The dark night yawned far and wide; the blacks, blues and grays swirling together and appearing as sort of an unnatural aurora borealis. The night glowed ever so slightly, but still remained dark. It was an enigma and something that you would only find here.

"What are you thinking, Love?" Cadmus murmured into my hair, before he kissed my forehead. I could feel the exact place where his lips had been even after he removed them.

"I'm just pondering the differences between Pasadena and here," I answered softly. "And how you have taken to this place with surprising panache. You make it look so easy. It is as though you never left."

"Well," he smiled. "It helps that I had no memory of who I was when I first arrived. Eris deposited me in her home and I truly remembered nothing of who I was or where I had come from. I just felt this... overwhelming sense of love for her. It was as though I had always been with her. But at the same time, it was confusing, because it was absolutely superficial. I couldn't think of any details surrounding our relationship... because there weren't any. I'm so happy to be back with you where I belong."

I sighed and snuggled closer.

"You don't wish you were back with Eris?" I asked teasingly. But then I stiffened as another thought occurred to me. "You didn't... I mean, you and Eris..." I raised nervous eyes to meet his.

"Honestly, I don't remember. I hope not. As soon as you brought me back to myself, all memories of that time with her were instantly gone. All I can remember now is the strange sensation that I felt the entire time I was with her. I can't explain it. It was as though a sort of fog had descended upon me. It must have been whatever spell she used."

I nodded, strangely satisfied by that answer. Whatever had happened, it wasn't his fault. And if he couldn't remember it... well, that was almost as good as not happening at all. At least, that was what I would tell myself.

As I situated myself even closer to Cadmus, something out of the corner of my eye caught my attention and I paused, scanning the dark night. On the edge of the circle of fire, just beyond the light, two eyes were staring at me. They fairly glowed in the darkness and I froze, my breath caught in my throat. Cadmus glanced down at me.

"What is it?"

I lifted a trembling finger and pointed at the same time as the eyes began moving toward me.

One breath later, a large black dog sat on the perimeter, calmly observing me as I tried not to panic. It very slowly lifted a paw and licked it, keeping its yellow eyes on me the entire time. This was not an ordinary dog. I could tell from the intelligent, human-like way it was staring at me. It was unsettling.

"What do you want?" I called to it. It was no more than ten feet away. Cadmus slowly rose to a crouch, drawing a dagger from his side. He stayed poised at my side, ready for anything.

The dog watched me silently for a moment more before it quickly morphed into Hecate. I breathed a sigh of relief and I felt Cadmus relax as he stood up and offered me his hand, pulling me to my feet.

Hecate smiled a patronizing smile.

"Why is it that you are so jumpy?" she asked. "Scared of a little dog?"

"I wouldn't call you little," I replied. "What is it that you want?"

"Aren't you going to say thank you, Harmonia? I gave you the tools to awaken your friends."

By this time, my 'friends', the Amazons, had formed behind me, every one of them ready to defend me if need be. I could feel the tension in the air and I addressed them without turning.

"It's okay, friends… I am sure Hecate means no harm. Do you, Hecate?" I raised my eyebrows.

"Of course not," she replied, her smile unwavering.

"And yes. We should thank you," I added. "You saved the night. We appreciate your efforts."

"Your gratitude is not why I am here," she replied brusquely. "I'm here to tell you something that you don't know. I saw a vision of Aphrodite. She wants you to find Ares before you come to her. She is safe, no harm has come to her. But she feels that you will need Ares in order to help her."

"How do you know this?" I asked uncertainly.

"I saw her, of course," Hecate answered matter-of-factly. "She's well, I assure you. But you must listen to me. You must do as she wishes and you must find Ares. He will help you save us all."

I took a shaking step backward. Save them all? I couldn't even save Aphrodite.

Hecate noticed my hesitation.

"I have foreseen that you will save us, Harmonia. It will be written in the stars for all of eternity. If you choose to act on your destiny, that is." She stared at me mockingly. "Will that be your choice?"

"Don't speak to me about destiny!" I said angrily. "For two thousand years, the Fates have manipulated me using that very same line. Destiny, fate. What are those things except for someone imposing their will on others?"

I felt anger bubbling to the surface and I fought to suppress it. It wouldn't do to lose my temper with her. Nothing here was her fault, even if her attitude was annoying at best.

She stared at me placidly, unmoved by my mini-rant.

"Do you expect me to feel sorry for you, Harmonia? Yes, you've been relegated to mortal form for a couple of millennia. Yes, your lives have been sad. So what? No one truly dies. Your soul is that of a goddess. Here you stand now in front of me in your true form no worse for the wear. What should I feel sorry for?"

Her eyes flashed fire for a brief moment and I wondered at her ire.

"I mean no disrespect toward you, Hecate," I murmured. "It is easy to become agitated at one's lot in life at times."

She nodded. "Yes," she agreed. "It is. But one must learn to overcome it. Self-pity is not helpful to anyone. Pull on your goddess panties, my dear. It's time to come out swinging."

Hecate wanted me angry. I could feel it. Perhaps she felt if I were angry, I would fare better against the Fates. And maybe she was right. If my back was up, I would be far less inclined to back down. But backing down wasn't in the cards for me. I could feel that much.

"Do you know where Ares is?" I asked, sticking my chin out.

She shook her head.

"No. They are very effectively blocking that information from us. We've tried Seeking spells, but to no avail. All we see is blackness when we try. You must find him, my dear. It is up to you."

"I thought you said I would need you two more times?" I asked suspiciously.

"And you will," she nodded. "That much is certain. And when you need us, we will be there. Do not doubt that."

"Thank you," I replied quietly. "I will ponder Ares' whereabouts. Perhaps it is something that I already know... that I just cannot remember. I feel so much lingering just under the surface of my memory. I just can't access it. It is maddening."

She nodded. "Yes. That is the result of the Fates. They have done that to us all, I am afraid. But we must overcome it. And we will, I assure you. Eventually."

She sounded so sure of herself and I wished I felt the same. Cadmus laid his hand on the small of my back as we watched her shift into the black dog's shape once more. She nodded her large head towards us in a gesture of farewell as her golden eyes glowed in the night.

And then she was gone.

I turned to Cadmus. "I don't know what to do. I don't know where to look. Everyone is counting on me and I might fail them all." I could hear the anxiety in my voice and so could he. He grasped my hands with both of his own and squeezed them gently.

"My love, I have never known you to fail. You have always accomplished whatever you needed to do."

My eyes flew to his.

"Do you remember everything now? All of the lives that we have shared?..." my voice trailed off. Could I be so lucky?

He nodded.

"I don't remember all of the details, but I do remember bits and pieces of so many of them. Mainly, I remember the feelings. The overwhelming feeling of love that I have always felt for you. It is almost tangible and it seems that it conquers everything, regardless of how much the Fates would wish it otherwise. They cannot stop what we feel."

And I realized that he was right. They couldn't. They could block our memories and they could make us fail to even remember who we were… but they couldn't erase what we felt for each other. Cadmus was a genius.

I leaned up and kissed him quickly on the cheek.

"Cadmus, my love, you are amazing. That is brilliant. Thank you!"

He raised a dark eyebrow.

"For?"

"For telling me what I need to do!" I called over my shoulder as I rushed back to the center of the circle. Digging through my bag, I pulled out the compass.

Ortrera gazed at me.

"Sister, you know it can't lead you to someone unless you can picture the location."

I stared back. "Maybe, but think on this… each of us harbors a place in our heart for those that we love. The love that we feel for everyone is different and unique. It is essentially a specific place. Couldn't that be used as some sort of a beacon for this compass to use in tracking someone?"

I concentrated on the globe, staring into it as I focused on the place in my heart where my father dwelled. I pictured him as Ares, massive and fearless, leading countless wars for Zeus. He had never been afraid of anything and had certainly never backed down. I pictured him as Marc Antony, laughing and strong, leading Cleopatra's armies against Rome. He was brave and gallant and tragically beautiful. The familiar feelings that I felt for him were overwhelming and always the same no matter what form he took.

And as I stared into the compass, he began to materialize before my eyes. Slowly and faintly, but he was there. I was doing it. I could see his outline and his dark hair. My pulse raced as I thought harder, pulling out every memory that I had. And the picture completed itself.

I gasped as I stared into his familiar face.

Ares was also my mortal father.

Chapter Thirteen

He had the muscled body of Ares, but his face still resembled Paul Lockhart's enough that I instantly recognized him. And I don't know why I was so surprised or how I hadn't noticed it before.

My father had left my mother for his secretary, he loved to flirt, he had bought me a Lexus. He loved extravagance and women- something that Aphrodite, in every life, tolerated. But this... this did take me off guard. I hadn't been expecting it, even if it did seem so obvious. In mortal terms, their age difference was disgusting.

Jade had just turned eighteen and my father was thirty-nine. But I had to push that aside. We weren't dealing with mortal terms or mortal rules now- because none of us was really mortal at all.

And really, none of this should surprise me. Ares was present in some form in every life I had ever led. He and Aphrodite always found each other, as did Aphrodite and myself...and Cadmus. We were all tied to each other. We were no longer Macy, Jade, Paul Lockhart or Gavin. Neither were we Cleopatra, Charmian, Marc Antony or Hasani. Not anymore.

We were all ageless. Time could no longer constrain us.

I sighed. Things just got more curious as time progressed.

I turned to Cadmus and the Amazons to relay the news. Their faces reflected the surprise that I was sure had been on my own.

"Now what?" Cadmus asked in amazement.

"Now I tell you the other part. He's here already. Look."

I thrust the compass toward him. Ares stood proudly in the center, his arms and legs restrained with heavy chains as Alexi stood at his side. In the background, I could see the dungeons of Zeus' palace. He was here in the Spiritlands on Olympus. No wonder he hadn't been at the hospital the night of homecoming and hadn't returned my mother's phone calls. He had been here. And he didn't look happy.

"Why did Hecate say that we needed to find Ares first, before we sought out Aphrodite?" Ortrera asked. "We should reach them at the same time. He's clearly at Olympus already."

"Perhaps Aphrodite is not," I suggested. Peering into the globe, I fervently conjured up every emotion I had ever felt toward my mother. I pictured her as Jade, Cleopatra, Aphrodite and everything in between and the love that I had felt for her each and every time. And she appeared.

She was lying on some sort of thick marble slab, her hands and feet bound with golden cords, her face indignant. Of course, the cords must be enchanted to hold a goddess and Aphrodite did not look pleased about being restrained. I almost laughed at the look of pure outrage on her lovely face, but it died in my chest when I saw who she was with.

Instead of Eris, whom I expected, someone else was standing over her left shoulder.

Annen.

The next thing I knew, Cadmus was gently picking me up off the ground, cradling me to his chest.

"Come back to me, love," he murmured into my ear. "I'm here. Come to me."

I had fainted. For a goddess, I certainly didn't contain my feelings very well. I opened my eyes and stared into his.

"Cadmus, something is so, so wrong. I don't know what to believe anymore. Annen is with Aphrodite. The Keres have her."

I slumped back against his chest and allowed him to hold me as I pondered this new twist. His heart clanged against his ribs and it soothed me with his rhythmic cadence. I zoned out completely for a few minutes, just trying to calm down and absorb this new knowledge. Finally, I lifted my head one more time.

"Why are they doing this?" I whispered. "What do they stand to gain?"

Cadmus shook his head. "I do not know," he admitted. "I think there is much that we do not yet know."

I nodded in agreement while Ortrera spoke up.

"Perhaps this is an instance where Hecate can help. Perhaps she knows or can help us sort it out."

"Perhaps," I murmured.

At this point, I didn't feel encouraged. I still felt blind-sided by the Keres' betrayal. I had been so thoroughly convinced that they meant to help me. Ahmose had even said as much at the pool before he died.

Something wasn't clicking. This couldn't be right. I couldn't force my mind to bend around this betrayal.

"In the morning, we will ride directly to the witches," Cadmus decided. "It cannot hurt to try."

The Amazons nodded their assent and we all settled down for the night. I lay inside the comfort of Cadmus' arms and stared blankly at the night as I listened to the sounds around me. Subtle movements from blankets scraping against skin, the crackling of the fire and then later, even the eerily haunting cry of a Chimera somewhere high above us. I didn't let it bother me. I simply moved closer to Cadmus, comfortable in the fact that any Chimera would have to go through him to get to me. And he had already slayed dragons.

* * *

We flew at dawn, when the sunrise was just staring to peek above the horizon of the Spiritlands. Yellowy fingers stretched across the land, bathing our faces in the warmth of the sun. I wished that I could ride with Cadmus and rest against his chest as we flew through the clouds, but it wasn't possible. I once again clutched Ortrera's back as I rode behind her in the front of the formation.

Below us, I could see inhabitants of the Spiritlands going about their daily lives. Just as in the real world, farmers farmed, merchants sold things, builders built. It was easier here, to be sure, because so many of the residents possessed magical abilities to some degree, but that was normal for this enchanted place.

After a time, I noticed that our horses were slowing the pulse of their wings. I glanced at Ortrera.

"They require nectar," she explained. "They haven't been able to drink in a while. They are growing tired."

As she scanned the landscape below us, I gazed at Cadmus. Had he managed to drink? Last night, he had brought me a flask, but I had not seen him drink from it. His appearance was just the same as it was as Gavin's, so it was likely that he had not. He would need it soon, also. No one could safely stay in mortal form for long here.

Ortrera spotted a stream and turned her horse's head towards it, the rest of the warriors following suit. We descended next to the water in a field of waving purple daisies. Like normal, before I could dismount, Cadmus was at my side pulling me from the horse. I felt his arms tremble as he held me, a tell-tale sign of fatigue.

I laid my hand against his cheek.

"Sweet, you haven't yet taken nectar. You must or you will grow weak here. I need you strong."

He nodded, his jaw flexing, and I wondered at his apparent reluctance. But I didn't remark on it. Instead, I watched him crouch by the stream and scoop it into his mouth. He swallowed with his beautiful eyes closed and his face tilted toward the sun.

While I watched, he transformed into the Cadmus from my memory. His muscles filled out, each individual striation in his biceps becoming apparent to the naked eye. His face quickly leaned down into that of a man, while still retaining his handsome, boyish good looks. I sucked in my breath. My god, he was beautiful. With the sun shining onto him from behind and the stream sparkling next to him, he truly seemed unworldly.

He had the strangest expression on his face and I stepped toward him in concern.

"My love," I began hesitantly. "What is it? Does something trouble you?"

He nodded curtly, remaining silent as a muscle in his jaw flexed.

"Well?" I prompted. "What is it? Do you feel unwell?"

He sighed and shook his head.

"No. I feel fine. But, Harmonia, the nectar restored my memory. I was afraid of that. I didn't wish to remember."

I was completely puzzled until a scant second later I realized what he meant.

"Your memories with Eris?" I whispered.

He nodded slowly.

"I don't wish to talk about it," he said softly. "There is no need to trouble you with it, too. Let us just remember that it wasn't truly me. I was enchanted, I wasn't myself. She...we... didn't. But it was enough." His voice choked off and he grabbed me in a fierce embrace, clutching me to him tightly.

"You are the one, Harmonia," he growled into my hair. "It is you. It has always been you. No matter what happened. Do you understand?"

The pain in his voice distracted me from my own dismay and I nodded silently. He was right. He could not help what happened any more than I could.

"Cadmus, do not trouble yourself with it. Put it out of your mind," I pleaded softly. "You are right. It wasn't you. I know that."

He nodded and turned away, busying himself with filling his flask. I gave him the alone time. I knew him inside and out. He needed to regroup. And I needed something to distract me, as well. If I focused on it, it might well become my undoing.

I turned to Ortrera. "I want her head on a spike, sister."

I should have been ashamed of the venomous thought, but I wasn't. Apparently, my goddess blood was colder than my mortal blood, something that could come in handy.

Ortrera nodded with a gleam in her eye and a smile.

"I don't blame you. And I will give that to you, if you wish. Just say the word."

I smiled in appreciation as I let my anger simmer toward my ancient nemesis. Truly, this time she had gone too far. I would restrain myself for now, but her time would come.

The warriors finished tending to their horses and we again mounted and took off for the witches. It was as though even the horses could sense our energy and anxiety. They tossed their mighty heads and nickered from time to time as they flew. I watched the Pegasus to my right with amusement. She seemed to keep an eye on me, gauging my reactions, reading my face. I smiled and I could almost swear that she rolled her large eye at me.

The witches' cave was on the edge of the Spiritlands and I kept my eyes trained for it as we drew closer. It wasn't a typical cave, even though it appeared that way on the outside. It was rumored that inside, it contained a direct passageway to the underworld. And that made sense, since one of Hecate's abilities was the ability to send demons to the underworld. Hades probably did grant her direct access.

I caught sight of it a few minutes later. I nudged Ortrera as I pointed and we aimed towards it, the formation moving as one. It was absolutely amazing- almost like the horses could communicate silently, coordinating each movement to match the horse to their side. For all I knew, that was exactly what they were doing. Nothing in the Spiritlands was impossible.

We landed soundlessly on the grounds right outside the cave, the horses' hooves as silent as they were trained to be. Even still, I wasn't surprised to find Hecate leaning against the cave opening, apparently waiting for us. Being the witch that she was, she had uncanny instincts.

"So, you came," Hecate drawled as we quietly approached her.

I nodded as I glanced inside. It was unlike any cave I had ever seen. Once inside the doorway, it opened into a massive cavernous room filled with sparkling white stalactites and stalagmites. Light bounced from each glistening crystal to the next, illuminating the entire cave. It was almost ethereal and certainly not what I had expected from the queen of witchcraft.

"How could I not?" I answered grimly. "I trusted the Keres. And they have betrayed me. I feel like I can no longer trust my instincts."

"And your birthmark?"

I glanced down and noticed in surprise that the phoenix birthmark that had marked me as a Keeper for generations had grown more pronounced. It was now a deep crimson, not unlike the color of henna. My startled gaze flew up to meet hers. She was already nodding knowingly.

"It has been silent since we arrived here, yet it has grown more pronounced," I stumbled over my words.

She nodded again.

"It is all true," she muttered to herself as she gestured for us to enter.

"What is true?" Cadmus asked, a note of concern in his husky voice.

"Your wife is the chosen one," Hecate confirmed. My heart started pounding. The crazy raven had said as much before he flew away when we first arrived. I had brushed it away at the time. But now...

"The chosen one?" I asked doubtfully.

"You are meant to save us," Hecate nodded. "It has always been you. You have the mark."

"Lachesis gave me this mark," I shook my head. "To mark me as a Keeper."

Hecate stared at me in disdain.

"Harmonia, when will you stop accepting people at face value? I realize it is in your nature to believe the best in people, to expect the best, but it simply isn't so in life. Lachesis lied to you. You are marked as the chosen one. It has nothing to do with the lies of the Moirae. They simply bewitched it to cause you pain when you went against their plans."

As she spoke, Hecate treaded further into the beautiful cave and we trailed behind. I gazed around us as we walked, taken aback by the beauty surrounding us. The light stone walls looked as though they had been formed from crushed jewels.

She walked to a massive wall of leather-bound books and chose one. As she flipped through the pages, I inhaled the scent of old paper as my mind whirled.

"Why me?" I murmured. "I am nothing great. I am just the daughter of greatness."

Hecate peered at me over the rim of the book.

"Why *not* you?" she asked. "Greatness often comes from unexpected places."

She turned the heavy book towards us and I leaned to take it. A vivid image of a woman surrounded by fire was painted on the ancient parchment. Her hair was long and dark, her eyes a brilliant, glowing green. On her wrist, was a crimson Phoenix. The color of the bird was the exact shade that my birthmark had become.

It was most certainly me. That much was unmistakable.

I was dumbfounded as I read the script below the picture.

She who will save Olympus and all that we know. Treacherous snakes will tremble beneath her fingers and the crown shall be restored.

I took a deep breath.

"So, Lachesis lied about the Keepers. There were never any more than just me?" It was difficult to wrap my mind around.

"Not so," Hecate corrected me. "There are other divine children, meant to act as Keepers of their parents' mortal enslavement. They acted as you did, enchanted in the same way. They each believed that they were keeping fate. They have no knowledge of who they are or what they are truly doing. But you are correct. They are not marked and they do not possess bloodstones. This is why you are special. The Fates have known this all along. They have always known that you are meant to be their undoing."

"Then why didn't they just kill me?" I asked. "They could have killed me when I was mortal and no one would have ever known."

She shook her head again as though confounded by my ignorance.

"Harmonia, you are a divine child. You cannot truly die except by Zeus' sword through your heart. Zeus managed to hide it when the Fates took over Olympus. No one has found it.

And the Moirae have looked everywhere. They have searched the world to no avail."

"Yet it must be somewhere," I pointed out.

"Correct," she nodded. "It must be somewhere. And the one who finds it will restore the throne."

She tapped the picture again. The first time I looked, I had been focused on the phoenix on my wrist. This time, however, I noticed my other hand. A heavy looking sword dangled from it. My breath froze on my lips.

Oh, Mary Mother of God. This just didn't get any easier. I was supposed to somehow free the Olympic gods from the treachery of the Moirae and do so by being a chosen one who would find a sword that no one else had managed to find in over two thousand years?

Perfect. I should have expected nothing less.

"You must retrieve your father," Hecate announced, watching me with her knowing eyes. "Do not doubt your abilities or your right. You are the chosen one. You must take what is yours."

I swallowed hard, then swallowed again. It was growing difficult to breathe in this room. I felt Cadmus step closer to me, stroking my shoulders lightly. Of course he would notice my distress. I kept my chin stuck out, hoping that no one else noticed.

Hecate extended her hand, her long fingers curled around something.

"Here," she uttered. "This is the second time you will need our assistance."

I looked at it suspiciously. "What is it?"

Nothing appeared to be moving in her hand, which was a good sign. There was also no foul smell. I gritted my teeth and held my hand out.

She dropped a brass key into my palm.

I studied it. It was just a simple brass key. It looked like a normal skeleton key that you might find in any old house. I looked at Hecate quizzically.

"There's a catch," she murmured. "You must dip it in your own blood before you attempt to use it. No one else's will work. It must be yours."

"Of course," I answered, rolling my eyes.

"Do you have the remainder of the Resurrection Potion that I gave to you?"

I nodded. "There is not a lot left, but there are a couple of drops."

"Good. Keep it. You will need it."

I briefly wondered who I would need it for before I put it out of my mind. There was no use pondering it. I didn't have the gift of prophecy and I wasn't a witch.

I sighed.

Hecate watched me in amusement. "My dear, it is no time to be weary. You have only just begun."

I stared at her. "Comforting."

She shrugged her shoulders and replaced the book on the shelf. Turning back around, she spoke again.

"Do you still have the Map of Souls?"

I nodded. "In my knapsack."

"You should leave it in my safekeeping, Harmonia. The Moirae would like it back and that wouldn't be in anyone's best interest."

I considered that, but before I could say anything, Cadmus spoke my thoughts exactly.

"How do we know that we can trust you, witch?"

She aimed a hard stare at him. "You don't. But you know that you can't trust the Moirae, now don't you?"

She had a point.

I dug through my knapsack and pulled out the Map of Souls, handing it to her.

"I was told to guard this with my life. So you should do the same," I instructed.

She nodded curtly at me and gestured toward her massive wall of tomes.

"I've got experience," she said wryly. I smiled for the first time since we had arrived. The witch had a sense of humor, something I hadn't noticed before.

"You need to go," she continued. "Free your father and find your mother. I have seen that you will have obstacles. Keep your head clear and you will outsmart them. Remember, greatness comes from unexpected places."

I nodded. It sounded so easy when she put it that way. Just keep my head clear and all would work out. Really? I knew better. Nothing was that easy.

We turned and filed out of the cave, Cadmus right on my heels and the Amazons behind him. We re-mounted, the Amazons turning the horses toward the mountain rising from the horizon.

Olympus.

Chapter Fourteen

$\mathcal{T}$he once magnificent city was deserted. Even the falcons stationed at the gates of the city were gone. It was eerie and unsettling. Not a glimpse of movement throughout the still streets. It was as though we were walking through a ghost town. We moved quickly until we stood at the base of the stairs leading to the palace.

I glanced at Cadmus and Ortrera.

"Where is everyone?" I asked uneasily.

Cadmus shook his head slowly as he gazed around us. "I have no idea."

A lone raven sat on the abandoned porch of a crumbling stone home nearby. I turned to it.

"Where has everyone gone?"

It simply stared at me, its crimson eyes gleaming in the light.

"Where has everyone gone?" I repeated, louder this time.

It opened its beak wide. Its tongue had been cut out. Just like Annen. I gasped. Why would they bother with a bird?

The warriors slapped the rumps of their horses and they took off into the sky, circling above us in a perfectly formed holding pattern. I knew they would return the moment that the Amazons' called for them.

As we climbed the stairs and entered the palace, the first thing I noticed was the horrible smell. Covering my nose with my hand, my gaze flew around the room to find the source of the foul odor. Sulfurous and acidic, the horrid smell seemed to penetrate my nasal tissue and cling there. Every breath I took tasted of it.

"Dragon," Cadmus murmured to us and his quiet voice seemed to echo in the empty building.

I looked at him, my eyebrows raised.

"Dragon?" I repeated nervously. He nodded.

"No doubt about it. This is their scent."

I sighed. "They need to shower."

He laughed and I marveled at his ability to find humor even as we faced such a dire circumstance. There was a dragon running loose here for Pete's sake.

We treaded carefully through the abandoned halls, carefully scanning every corridor before we entered it. There was still no movement and no sign of a dragon. Normally, I would be relieved. But I knew that it was here somewhere and I would rather face it now then continually wonder when it would appear.

Crossing a great room, I pulled Achilles' Shield out from where it was half-concealed beneath a lounge. It was very strange that the Moirae didn't take it or at the very least hide it better. It would benefit them greatly in the case of a fight. I gulped as I realized that they didn't think it would go that far. They thought this would be an easy victory for them.

I handed the heavy shield to Cadmus and then glanced at the others.

"Stay clear of Atropos," I warned. "She can suck your life away if you get too close."

They nodded as we crept forward.

Searching the main floor of the palace proved to be anticlimactic. There was simply no one here. It was as quiet as a tomb. We stared at each other uncertainly.

"The dungeons," I murmured.

Ortrera looked around warily as we descended the marble stairs.

"You know this is a trap," she pointed out.

"Yes. But we have no choice," I replied. And we didn't. Whatever happened would happen.

Turning the corner at the base of the stairs, we entered a long corridor that led to the dungeons. With every step we took, the rancid smell grew stronger. The dragon was down here. And it could probably smell us coming. I found it strangely ironic that as horrible as they smelled, they had the keenest senses of smell on the planet. Like a shark in the water, they could sense prey from a mile away. I shuddered

Cadmus gripped my hand for a moment.

"We will be alright, my love," he assured me. "Just stand behind me. I have the shield."

He stepped ahead of me and for the time being, I allowed it. I would never allow him to endanger his life for me, though, not as he had in Alexandria when he almost died to save me. I couldn't go through that again.

By the end of the hall, the air was so ripe with the stench that it was literally difficult to breathe. Regardless, I took a steadying, deep breath before we pushed open the massive wooden doors that led to the inner dungeons.

A dragon loomed in front of us, practically filling the entire cavernous chamber. Massive and dark yellow, its eyes were wild as it watched us. It was covered in serpent-like scales and easily weighed several tons. It had delicate looking wings folded at its sides, red and paper thin. I could see the black veins through the membrane-like skin.

As I stood observing it, I could feel its fetid breath flaring out of its nostrils and moving the hair on my forehead. And I froze. I knew it could breathe fire. Behind it, Ares hung limply from the ceiling, bound at the hands and feet. His eyes were closed and his head was slumped against his chest. I could see his chest barely moving. I sighed a small sigh of relief. He still breathed.

The dragon took one awkward step toward us, the tip of its tail twitching like a cat's. The tension was unbearable. It was like we were suspended in time, each waiting for the other to act.

And then it did.

Unexpectedly, it reared back on its enormous hind legs and threw its head back, exhaling a gust of fire from across the room. We lunged behind Cadmus as he blocked us with Achilles' Shield. The fire was diverted off of the impenetrable surface, flowing instead to the stone ceiling of the dungeon where it fizzled harmlessly and went out.

I could smell scorched fabric and singed hair, but none of us were harmed. I locked eyes with Cadmus. His chocolate eyes stared pointedly at me.

"Trust me," he murmured.

Before I could even react, he thrust the shield at me and lunged to the side, rolling beneath another scorching breath of fire and vaulting himself away from the dragon's dangerous mouth. I screamed for him, but he didn't look back.

I watched his lithe limbs move gracefully as he danced away from the dragon's face. I couldn't help but admire his agility. He was born to be a warrior. I clenched my teeth so that I didn't scream again and distract him. The entire time, I wondered what his plan was. How did one conquer a dragon? Although, he had done it before, a fact I silently repeated to myself in order to remain calm.

The dragon's scales glistened in the light as it watched Cadmus with golden, reptilian eyes. Every few seconds, the thick membrane that covered its eye twitched, an outward sign of its annoyance with us.

"Aim!" Ortrera called from behind me.

I glanced over my shoulder to find the Amazons squatting tensely with their bows poised. Thin arrows tipped with bronze were aimed at the dragon, half at its head, half at its heart. Cadmus rolled to the side as Ortrera called, "Release!"

The arrows flew in graceful arcs toward the dragon, each one falling away impotently. The sharp arrows might as well have been pixie sticks or dull pencils. They simply couldn't penetrate the dragon's leather-like skin. Dejection started to form in my belly and I thrust it away. There had to be something we could do.

Racing to the edge of the room, I threw open the doors of a nearby cabinet. Inside, hung several odd torture devices. A mace, strange looking long screws, sharp hammers and a rusty sword. Wrestling the sword from the brackets constraining it, I lugged it several steps. My muscles ached from the effort. It was incredibly heavy.

"Cadmus," I cried. He locked eyes with me and nodded from halfway across the room.

I gathered my strength and concentrated on focusing my efforts. I pictured my inner strength pooling in my arms, building with each heart beat. I felt it pulsing with each breath. Growing. With a shriek, I released my pent up goddess strength. Like a rubber band, it flexed and broke free. Catapulted by my super-human effort, the sword flew perfectly into Cadmus' hands.

I slumped to the floor, spent by my effort. My limbs were weak and shaky. Drawing on goddess strength was an intense experience.

Cadmus effortlessly handled the iron sword, bending and swaying to avoid the dragon's harmful breath. I flattened myself against the wall- I was too far away to enjoy the benefits of the shield.

"Cadmus," Ortrera called.

He glanced her way and she hefted the shield toward him. He caught it in his left hand, the sword still in his right. I concentrated on my breathing. It wouldn't help anything to hyperventilate. With the safety of the shield gone, the Amazon warriors quickly rolled out of the dungeon and back into the safety of the hall. My gaze flew back to my soul mate.

He danced gracefully in front of the dragon, shifting his weight from the ball of one foot to the other. His hands didn't falter or shake. He was calm and his gaze was deadly. I realized that I had stopped breathing and I took a deep breath. It also wouldn't help anything if I passed out from lack of oxygen.

I glanced behind the dragon once more and Ares still hung limply and unmoving. I had a feeling that time was running short.

"We need to hurry, Cadmus," I cried. "Ares can't hold on much longer."

Cadmus nodded silently, keeping his intense gaze on the beast in front of him.

The dragon's large eyes rotated and fixed on Cadmus, while dark steam poured from its nose. It pawed at the floor with its webbed front claws, pluckily moving from one side to the other like it was prepared to lumber in either direction.

"Harmonia?" Cadmus called, without taking his focus from the beast in front him.

"Yes?" I answered.

"Get down!"

I dropped to the floor in a balled up crouch, instinctively covering my head with my hands. Peeking from around my arms, I watched as Cadmus dropped the shield and used it as a platform to lunge from. He rocked on it backward, then bounced off the front, flying through the air toward the reptile.

In response, the dragon roared a mouthful of fire, but it was too slow.

The fire spread to the walls and ceiling in a flattened out cloud, but Cadmus was already in front of the flame and rocketing toward the dragon's head. Looping one strong leg around the dragon's neck, he landed astride the writhing animal. Heaving the heavy sword, he plunged it deep into the side of its neck.

The beast froze with one more strangled cry. Its roving eye found mine and with its gaze locked onto me, it fell to the ground. The dungeon shook with its weight as it landed. I literally felt the earth between my feet move. I looked back at the dragon and saw its sides heaving as it struggled to breathe. Black blood ran down the side of its neck and pooled on the ground beside it.

Its chest shuddered, then stopped.

It was dead.

I uncrouched and launched myself toward Cadmus, leaping into his arms, completely disregarding the fact that he was covered in black dragon's blood. I covered his face in kisses, clinging to his neck.

"Oh, my god, oh my god," I muttered as I clung to him. "Don't ever do that to me again. I almost had a heart attack. It could've killed you."

He rolled his eyes.

"Woman, I'm not a novice. I've killed dragons before."

"Thousands of years ago!" I exclaimed. "You're out of practice."

"Are you doubting my skills?" he asked with a raised eyebrow.

I looked at the dead dragon to our side and shook my head.

"Never. You are a warrior, through and through."

"Well, I'm glad you realize that," he acknowledged.

I slid from his grasp and raced around the hulking frame of the dragon. Ares was suspended from a weird pulley of sorts from the ceiling. I hurriedly looked for the lever that controlled it.

"It's over here," Cadmus called from the other side of the dragon. I abandoned my search and joined him just as the Amazons re-entered the chamber.

"That was foolish," Ortrera observed to Cadmus. "I approve," she smiled.

I rolled my eyes. Warriors.

Cadmus pulled the lever, slowly releasing Ares from the ceiling. The thick chains creaked as they moved and I raced to his side, helping Cadmus lower him gently to the ground.

Ares lay curled on his side, his thick black hair curling around his neck. They had clearly given him nectar for some reason or another. He had regained his god-like appearance. He reminded me strongly of Marc Antony now. His muscles bulged, his shoulders were wide. His mouth was full and slack as he rested.

"Ares, wake up," I rustled his arm. "Please, wake up."

The manacles constraining his thick wrists caught my eye and I remembered the key. I quickly slipped the knapsack from my back and dug through it, coming up with the brass key.

And then froze. I needed to dip it in my own blood.

"Cadmus," I began. He knelt by my side. "Your dagger, please."

His gaze flew to my face. "No."

"Yes," I replied. "I must. It will only be a small cut."

He wordlessly handed me his black-handled dagger and grasped my shoulder as he waited. I felt him stop breathing as he held his breath. I knew he couldn't bear to watch me injure myself, so I did it quickly.

In a quick movement, I sliced an inch long cut into my forearm. Blood instantly gushed and I rolled the key in it. I wryly hoped that the key was clean, although it was probably unlikely that a goddess would get an infection.

Slipping the key into the lock, I turned it. It clicked and the manacles fell to the side. I briskly rubbed Ares' arms, trying to stimulate his circulation. His forearms looked blue.

All of us were crowded around him, murmuring and trying desperately to rouse him. But to no avail. He stayed limp and still. I felt my pulse racing. He couldn't die. I couldn't let that happen.

"The potion," Ortrera reminded me. "Remember that you still have the potion. Hecate said you would need it once more."

I breathed a sigh of relief. Of course. The potion. Ortrera dug it out of my bag for me and handed it to me. I dipped the dropper into the silver bottle. Sure enough, there were only two drops left. Just as I started to drop them into his mouth, Ares' dark eyes opened.

He stared at me in confusion.

"Why are you here, daughter?"

His arms curled around me and I collapsed onto his chest, sobbing in wild relief.

"I thought you were dead," I mumbled against his blood-stained clothing. "I thought they had killed you."

I felt him smile against my forehead.

"What little faith you have in me," he murmured.

I could hear so much of Marc Antony in his voice that it warmed my heart. It was a myth that Ares was bloodthirsty and cruel. He was actually funny and kind-hearted, but just as he was as Marc Antony, he was still a warrior through and through. He could be bloodthirsty if need be. He would do whatever it took.

I sat up and twisted the lid back onto the potion and tossed it back into my bag. Hecate had been wrong. I hadn't needed it after all. Not that I was complaining.

Ares sat up, rubbing his bruised and battered body.

"The Moirae will wish they were dead when I am through with them," he muttered, scowling. He looked around at the faces surrounding him.

"Where's your mother?" he asked, turning to me. "Where's Aphrodite?"

I hesitated. He raised his eyebrow.

"Well?" he asked impatiently. "Where is she?"

"They have her," I answered quietly. "And I don't know exactly where."

His roar almost brought down the palace.

Chapter Fifteen

"*No*," Ares insisted again. "I have no memory at all of living in the mortal world. Nothing. I don't remember you as a mortal, I don't remember being a mortal, I don't remember being married to a mortal."

He paused and stared at me. "Does your mother know?"

I couldn't help but grin. My father, the god of war, was intimidated by Aphrodite, the goddess of love. Talk about ironic. But to be fair, she did have a colorful temper.

I shook my head. "Of course Aphrodite knows. But she's not mad," I assured him.

You could see the relief on his face as he gingerly stretched his limbs.

We were seated in a semi-circle in one of the Palace's many lounges. The building was a wreck. We'd had to clear a place out even to sit. It literally looked as though a hurricane had hit this place.

Ares drummed his fingers on the surface of a stone end table, absently staring out the window. Below us, the ravaged, deserted city of Olympus stood proudly. Even in ruins, it was hauntingly beautiful as the white stone buildings rose from the horizon out of the rustling velvety tree tops. Ares' face was impassive as he thought, but I knew him very well. He was planning a strategy.

Cadmus strode from the windows to reclaim his place at my side.

"What do you think, Ares?" he asked quietly. "Where have they taken Aphrodite?"

Ares shook his head in frustration. "I know not. And that vexes me."

He slammed his heavy fist onto the stone table, shattering it into a million pieces. They fell into a pile on the floor. Sadly, the pile of rubble fit in perfectly with our tattered surroundings.

I stepped to his side, resting my hands on his shoulders. "Calm yourself," I murmured. "Such tantrums won't help."

He scowled at me.

"Tis' easy for you to say. You're not the one who will answer to your mother. She expects a prompt rescue from me, I'm certain."

"Well, you *are* the god of war," I pointed out wryly, then smiled at his expression. "Calm yourself. We'll find her. We just have to think of places to look."

"I know where," a tiny voice sounded out, clear as a little bell.

We all startled and looked around. A tiny child was hidden in a pile of rubble across the room. She was so dirty that she blended right in. We'd all walked right past her without noticing her presence. But I could see her little pixie face peering out at us now. She couldn't be more than six or seven years old.

The Amazons jumped to attention, circling her warily. I gestured for them to stand down.

"Sister, it's merely a child," I assured Ortrera, edging up to stare at the girl. Ortrera clucked.

"You don't know that. The Moirae can shapeshift."

"True," I admitted. "But I don't think that is the case here. I feel like she is an innocent."

I knelt in front of her.

"Are you?" I asked her. "Are you an innocent?"

The little girl nodded, her plump pink lips trembling. I could tell that under the dirt smudges, she was a flawlessly beautiful child. Her skin was like porcelain, her hair was long and blonde and her eyes were cornflower blue. She looked like a perfect china doll, but for the dirt and bedraggled clothes.

"I know where they took her," she repeated. "Can you help me get back home?"

I held out my hand to her and she climbed from the wreckage of the furniture that she was hiding in. She stood uncertainly, watching the Amazons in fear.

"They won't hurt you," I assured her. "They are mighty warriors, but they are here to help."

"You're Harmonia, aren't you?" the child asked, her lip shaking.

I nodded. "How did you know?"

She pointed at my wrist. "Your mark. They were talking about it, too."

"The Moirae?" I asked with my eyebrows raised. I subconsciously found myself gripping my wrist and I forced myself to release it.

She nodded.

"What is your name, child?" I asked, all while trying to calm my racing heart.

It was astounding that this was all about me. I could hardly fathom the fact that it had never been about my Daedal. In fact, Daedals weren't even real things... They were just a ruse made up by the Fates. It was so hard to comprehend that the entire past two thousand years had been wasted. I shook the troublesome thoughts from my head and waited for the girl's name.

"Raquel," she answered nervously. "I live on Calypso's island."

"Why are you here?" I asked curiously. "You're quite a ways from home."

She nodded again, her blue eyes filling with tears. A single tear dripped down her dirty cheek.

"I miss it."

"Of course you do," I soothed, pulling her into my arms. "Anyone would. I miss my mother. Do you know where she is?"

The girl nodded. "That is why I am here. I'm supposed to tell you. Will you take me back with you?"

"Take you back? Do you mean to say that my mother and the Moirae are on Calypso's Island?"

The girl nodded and my gaze flew to Cadmus' over her head.

Ogygia, the island of Calypso, was an island that the Fates had long used as a 'holding place' of sorts. They marooned unknowing travelers there, and no one could leave until the Fates allowed it. People became sucked into the beauty of the island and time faded away. It was a beautiful paradise. The catch, however, was that it was a virtual 'no magic zone.' Magical abilities were rendered useless on Ogygia soil. Gods were as mortals, with no special gifts.

"Why would they do this?" I asked the others. "It will level the playing field and even they will be rendered impotent. Why would they do that to themselves?"

"There is something that has been bothering me ever since you explained this whole mess," Ares said. "The Moirae held me, the Keres held your mother. They wanted you to think that they are enemies... that the Keres broke away from them years ago. But what if that was not the case?"

I raised an eyebrow. "Meaning?"

"Meaning... What if they did break apart but they reunited for this cause. In which case, they would be wary of each other- distrustful."

"Which is why they would want to meet on a level playing field." I finished for him. "They want to level *each other* impotent. That's brilliant, Ares."

He shrugged. "I'm good at many things."

I rolled my eyes. Modesty wasn't one of those things. I mentioned as much and he grinned. Stretching out one of his long arm, he yanked me to him and crushed me against his side.

"I've missed you, you know," he told me. "You've got sass. You get that from your mother."

Ortrera rolled her eyes. She had never been much for familial bantering. She was pretty much a no-nonsense sort of person. But she was certainly effective that way.

"Focus, people." Ortrera asked. "We must prepare before we walk into their trap. Because you know they will have a plan."

"In order to form a strategy, we need to figure out what they have to gain," Cadmus interjected. "Why would the Keres and the Moirae reunite with so much bad blood between them?"

I pondered that.

"Because they feel like together they are invincible?" I wondered. "Separate, they are weaker, which would leave room for us to regain Zeus' throne. But together, they feel they are stronger than we are. Do you think that could be it?"

Ares nodded slowly. "That is all I can come up with as well. There is nothing else I can think of." He turned and surveyed the vast damage to Olympus through the open windows. "Olympus must be set right," he mused. "This is a tragedy."

Everyone nodded in agreement. We had all disagreed with Zeus on more than one occasion, but he had certainly never run the Spiritlands into the ground as the Moirae and Keres had.

"You know," I pondered. "Ahmose tried to alert me, I think. I think he disagreed with their actions and he told me to listen to what Annen had told me. Annen had already planted doubts in my head about my role as a Keeper. But I think he was doing that to lead me here. It was a ruse. He was pretending to hate the Moirae, when of course he was truly working with them. They wanted me here so that we could have this out once and for all."

"What does that have to do with Ahmose?" Ortrera asked.

"He died because he tried to warn me. At least, in his own way, he did. He told me to seek out Annen- it was like he was trying to tell me that they were together. But he couldn't tell me in actual words because the Moirae had rendered him silent."

"He's fortunate that they didn't cut out *his* tongue," Ortrera remarked wryly.

"Not so much," I replied. "They tortured him and burned him alive instead. I don't want that to be for nothing. We need to think of a plan."

"I'm way ahead of you," Ares muttered.

He turned back over a table and picked up several small broken pieces of furniture. Using them as battle pieces, he and Cadmus plotted our entry onto the island. I watched them murmur back and forth for a moment before turning to my half-sister.

"Ortrera, our father isn't considering one important factor. We will have no powers on Ogygia. Plus, without the Fates secluded in the Spiritlands like they used to be, there will be no one to draw us safely back off the island. We will be sucked into the enchantment. We will eventually forget our purpose there and wander around care-free."

She nodded. "I know. I've been considering that. Perhaps we should stop at the witches one last time on the way."

"Maybe. Perhaps this is the third time they will assist us," I suggested.

I noticed her warriors restlessly eyeing one another behind Ortrera. They didn't speak, but their body language said it all.

"You don't wish to go to the island, do you?" I asked them.

The one in front shook her head. "Something doesn't feel right about it. I know not what."

"I know," I agreed. "Being led into a trap set by the Fates is terrifying. But we have no choice."

Ares and Cadmus were wrapping up their strategy discussion and as I gazed at their backs, I felt a rush of warmth. Standing the way they were right now, if Cadmus' hair was just a bit longer and straighter, they could easily be mistaken for Antony and Hasani. The knowledge that we never really die had never seemed more real or relevant than right now and that actually bolstered my courage. We had survived so many other lives in order to stand here now. No matter what we faced, we would do it together. And I had faith that we would persevere.

Walking to Cadmus' side, I snaked my arm around his waist and leaned up to brush a kiss on his cheek.

"Are we ready?" I asked softly. He leaned down to press his soft lips to mine. Leaning back, he brushed my hair from my face, his hand cool.

"We are," he answered. "But you won't be going."

"What?" I asked in amazement. "Of course I am going. You need me to be there."

"Why?" Ares turned to me. "Explain why we would need you since everyone will be rendered the same once we arrive. Your bloodstone will be useless. Neither of us will have our powers. I see no point in endangering you. Clearly it's a trap. I don't wish for you to fall into it, too."

Raquel spoke up hesitantly.

"I forgot to tell you that part."

We all turned to her. She looked as if she wished she could melt into the floor.

"Lachesis wanted me to tell you that if you did not come, Aphrodite would suffer the same fate as Ahmose. They cannot kill her without Zeus' sword, but they will torture her and burn her... over and over."

I gulped.

"Is that reason enough for you?" I asked Ares.

My shoulders slumped. To even hear the threat of someone torturing my mother... it was chilling. Her faces all swirled together in my mind... Jade, Aphrodite...even Cleopatra's kohl-lined eyes as they crinkled when she laughed. Aphrodite loved to laugh. All of those images swirled around in my heart and I almost crumpled to the floor in my instant panic.

We had to save her.

"Let us go," I murmured. "We need to reach her. Now."

Ares shook his large head. "No. We will stay the night here in the city and travel to the island in the morning. We'll stop on the way to visit with Hecate." He looked at me drolly. "I'm not an idiot, daughter. Of course I considered the lack of magic on the island."

I smiled sheepishly at him before I turned to Raquel.

"Come with me, child. I will show you where I used to play here in the palace when I was your age. Did you know that I grew up here? I know every nook and cranny of this building."

I froze.

"I know every nook and cranny of this building," I repeated softly. "Ahmose knew that. I think he left something here for me," I exclaimed with excitement. "I don't know how I know it, I just do."

"Where should we look?" Ortrera asked.

"Everywhere," I answered.

We split up to search the palace for whatever it was that Ahmose might have hidden for me. Cadmus and Ares took the dungeons. The Amazons split up two to each floor. And I led Raquel with me as I sought out my old nursery.

No one else knew where I was headed, but I felt certain that I would be the one to find what we sought. In the back of the palace's nursery, there was a hidden room. Filled with crystals of every shape and size, it was the most beautiful and magical sight when light flooded the room. Rainbows shone on every surface. It was a magical place for a child to play. I had spent hours there when I was small. It had been a gift to the children of the palace from Zeus himself.

When we reached the doorway, we paused and I heard Raquel suck in her breath. And it truly was breathtaking. Every color of the rainbow ricocheted from every surface in the room. Magical toys lined glass shelves and I picked up a doll that I had played with when I was young, an exact replica of my mother. It was as new- it didn't appear to be over two thousand years old, which just drove home the fact that everything in the Spiritlands was timeless.

I sank to the floor on my knees with the doll clasped in my lap as I gazed around the room, my eyes flitting from one thing to the next. A rocking Pegasus, an ivory piano, a little bag of magic beans. I fondly remembered planting one outside of the palace and waiting for it to grow. My gaze froze and shifted back. Something was out of place.

A small black box sat on the bottom shelf. I innately knew that it wasn't meant to be there.

Crawling on all fours, I crossed to it and picked it up. The box was made from some sort of shiny black stone, maybe agate. A rolled up piece of parchment was lying on the top. It was waiting for me to find it. I could just feel it.

With Raquel at my side, peering over my shoulder, I unrolled the parchment. Ahmose's dark scrawl filled the page. My eyes welled up at the familiar sight, but I brushed my tears away impatiently. Now was not the time.

Harmonia,
You were always meant to be the one.
I apologize, my dear, for leading you astray for so long. It was not something I could change.
You have the knowledge to save everyone. I never stripped you of the memory that you will need, I allowed you to hide it away time and time again. I knew you would need it someday. Call on it when you are ready. This box will help you also. Use caution. It contains the soul of every murderous soul that the Keres ever claimed. These souls would enjoy vengeance.
Forgive me.

I allowed the parchment to fall to the floor as I absorbed what the Aegis had written. I felt sorry for the old priest, not anger. I felt certain that the priests on both sides, Annen included, were simply pawns enslaved and used by the Moirae and Keres. They had no choice but to comply.

I slid my hands over the glossy surface of the box. It seemed so sinister. Even without knowing what the box contained, I would have felt the ominous presence surrounding me as I held it. I wished I could destroy it or leave it... but we could not. Instead, I made sure the clasp was tightly fastened and I stuck it under my arm. The knowledge that so many murderers were contained so close to me was unsettling.

Raquel and I hurried back to the great room to wait for the others to return. It didn't take long.

Cadmus quickly crossed the room to me.

"Did you find anything?" he questioned.

I nodded. "Yes, but it is a riddle. Apparently, I have knowledge that will save us, but I don't remember it right now. I will focus on trying to retrieve the memory as we travel to the island."

"We'll leave first thing in the morning," Ares announced. "So think quickly, daughter. We cannot leave your mother there any longer or she will kill us all when we arrive."

I had to smile at the thought. There was no doubt that she would be annoyed at our tardiness.

The Amazon warriors struck out from the palace to gather lotus blossoms and nectar for us to dine on before we retired for the evening. I felt better immediately upon eating, refreshed and revived, as the nectar replenished my strength. I stood on the great room's balcony with a delicate golden goblet in my hand and observed the sunset as Cadmus wrapped his arms around me from behind.

I melted against his hard frame.

"Are you growing tired yet, my love?" he asked softly as he nuzzled the side of my neck.

I smiled. "Not *too* tired, sweet."

He grinned back. "Correct answer."

He grasped my hand and led me upstairs to the bedchambers.

Chapter Sixteen

I knew when the sun had come up because the orange-ish glow slanted across my face heralding the arrival of morning. I squinted my eyes and threw my arm over my brow. As I did, I noticed that the bed beside me seemed oddly empty. I quickly opened my eyes.

Cadmus was gone.

I felt panic bubbling up as I called for him. There was no answer. I called again.

Little Raquel appeared in the doorway. She had bathed and combed her hair and watched me nervously.

"They're gone," she murmured. "They said that would come back to get us."

I knew it. Anger formed in my belly and boiled upward. How dare they think they could leave me?

"All of them?" I asked. She nodded.

"The Amazons, too?" She nodded again.

When I found them, I might strangle them all. I pushed off of the bed and quickly readied myself as Raquel watched quietly. I turned to her.

"You need clean clothes, little one. Here." I waved my hand toward her and she was instantly wearing fresh clothing.

"Thank you," she murmured as she smoothed the skirt of her blue frock. "What will we do?"

"What anyone would do. We call for a witch."

I strode to the balcony and threw open the doors.

"Hecate!" I screamed into the empty city. "I need you!"

She had said that when I needed her, she would come. I needed her now.

When I turned from the balcony, she was standing in the doorway of the bedchambers, with Circes and Medea lingering behind her.

"You rang?" she asked with a smile. I scowled.

"They left me here. All of them. They're heading for Calypso's island without me."

Hecate shook her head. "Foolish, foolish men," she muttered. "They need you to prevail."

"I told them that," I agreed. "But they didn't listen."

"Men usually don't," she replied with a shrug.

"I need to get to Calypso's Island," I told her. "How do I do that?"

She stared at me in exasperation. "You are a goddess. You can do anything you wish."

"But I don't remember how!" I cried in frustration. "When will my memories be restored in full?"

"When you regain the crown," she answered simply. "Until then, you'll have to muddle through. This is not an instance where you require my assistance."

That was not the answer I was wanting. I scowled at her.

She sighed. "Where do you want to go?"

"I already told you- to Calypso's island!"

"Well, then, focus on it."

I wrinkled my brow as I considered that.

"Don't glare at me. Just focus on the island."

I did as she instructed and focused on the lush beaches of Ogygia. The water surrounding it was tranquil and blue. Palm trees framed the horizon as the sun hung low in the sky. I pictured Calypso herself swaying toward me in the evening breeze. I could practically feel the night air brush against my skin when all of a sudden, I felt myself leaving this room. I literally felt as though I was fading out of the palace. I held my arm up to find that it was becoming transparent.

I startled and suddenly, the feelings were gone. My body was back to normal, as solid as ever.

Hecate nodded in satisfaction. "You almost did it. Focus harder and next time, you will be there."

"Thank you," I murmured.

I turned to Raquel. "Little one, you must go with the witches. I do not wish to take you to a battle. When it is over, we will return for you and take you home."

She stared at me apprehensively.

Hecate extended her hand. "Come, child. Regardless of what you may have heard, I do not bite." Raquel hesitantly took a step toward her and grasped her hand.

"Tell me, do you like black dogs?" Hecate asked.

Glancing over her shoulder, she instructed, "Don't tarry."

And they were gone. I stood alone in the abandoned palace at the summit of Olympus. I had never felt so alone. Gripping my bloodstone, something that had been a constant in my life for a couple of millennia, I once again pictured the island. I knew that once I arrived, all magical abilities would be rendered useless. I would have to trust that whatever memory I had buried, whatever vague thing that was so valuable and hidden to me, would resurface and come to our aid.

Taking a deep breath, I pictured the sparkling water and the beach of the island. I focused on the feels, the smells... and suddenly my body faded away. It simply felt as though my limbs were falling asleep. And I was there. My feet were planted firmly in the sand. I wriggled my bare toes, scrunching them in the soil of the island. From this point on, I would be as a mortal.

I tucked my bloodstone into my tunic and gazed around me. Calypso swayed toward me from the other end of the beach. Her long red hair was flowing down her back, her skin as creamy as milk. Just as in my vision, the sun dipped low in the sky behind her, even though it was only morning in Olympus. Time was truly irrelevant here. Like everything else, it was rendered useless.

'Harmonia!" Calypso called. "Thank goodness you have arrived. I have grown weary of being a hostess. These visitors are quite demanding."

She reached me and pulled me into a quick embrace. She smelled of tropical flowers and vanilla. I could see why so many men had fallen victim to her charms- even her scent was intoxicating. She pulled away and grasped my hand.

"Come," she urged. "I will show you the way."

"Calypso, has anyone else arrived?" I asked hopefully.

She shook her head. "Not that I know of. Are you expecting someone?"

"Yes. My father, Cadmus and Ortrera's warriors should be along shortly. Once they arrive, please send them along."

"Of course I will," she answered agreeably. "Is Cadmus handsome?"

I shot her a look. "Don't even think of it. Cadmus is mine."

She sighed daintily. "Pity." Her eyes fluttered to my face. "But is he handsome?" she asked hopefully. "You know that men fall in love with me here."

I rolled my eyes. Calypso got lonely out here by herself, with only her servants for company. I couldn't quite blame her.

"Don't count on that," I replied good-naturedly. She grinned and focused once again on the path in front of us.

As she led me along through the manicured pathways and beautiful landscapes of the island, she chattered incessantly, grateful for a friendly visitor. I wasn't even listening, but she couldn't tell the difference. She hadn't let me get a word in edgewise.

She snagged my attention, though, when she said, "They're here to kill you, you know."

She said it so casually and matter-of-factly, as though she was speaking of the weather. I nodded.

"I know. They can certainly try."

"I'm fairly sure they are going to," she agreed. "Try, that is. You'll have to be very sneaky to avoid it."

"I can be sneaky," I replied with determination. Couldn't I? I would have to be.

"Calypso, can I ask you a question?" I looked at her hopefully. "With everyone on this island, how will I get back off? I didn't leave anyone on the mainland to retrieve me."

She clapped her hands joyfully. "Harmonia, that is wonderful. You can stay here with me forever!" She looked forlornly around us. "It's beautiful here but I do get lonely." She perked up. "But not if you stay. We'll have such fun! We'll be as sisters!"

"Calypso, don't get carried away. If I can possibly manage it, I will be leaving this island."

She nodded, but her expression was still hopeful. I rolled my eyes as I surveyed our surroundings. We were in a garden of some sort, surrounded by tropical flowers and white marble statues. Zeus stood mightily in the center with water spraying from his staff and falling into the fountain around him like rain. Hera sat gracefully in white marble on the ledge of the fountain, her expression fixed lovingly upon her husband. I gulped as I wondered where the Fates had imprisoned the King and Queen of the gods.

"Where are the Fates?" I murmured nervously to Calypso.

She paused her footsteps and turned back to me, her flowing skirt clinging to her legs in the breeze.

"They're in the center of the island," she whispered anxiously, looking all around us. "And Lachesis scares me."

"She scares me, too," I admitted. "But they are all pretty frightening."

"It's the strangest thing," Calypso continued, "They have made a strange sort of encampment in the center of the island. The Keres are in one bunker and the Moirae are in another. They have not mingled. But they are all waiting for the same thing. You."

She stared at me. "Why are you so important to them, Harmonia? I am isolated on this island. I do not know the current events."

"You are blessed to be so," I assured her. "Apparently, I am meant to save the enslaved gods. Don't ask me how, because I don't know yet."

"You'd better think quickly," she retorted. "You don't have long to plan."

"I know."

We continued walking through the entangled vines and trees until we came to a circular clearing, not unlike the clearing in the woods outside of Pasadena. I felt a strange sense of déjà vu as I stood in the center, gazing at the tropical trees encircling us.

The air was quiet and still, not even a breeze, so the grasses beneath our feet were calm. The sense of tension was palpable in the air, as if even the trees knew that something formidable was coming. We had walked quite a ways, so I felt certain that we were very close to the center of the island which is where the Moirae and Keres waited for me.

"Don't forget…if you lose, it will not be all bad. You can linger here with me and live forever," Calypso murmured.

I ignored her words. "Why are we here… in this place?"

I turned to her, but she was gone.

She had slipped from my side as silently as a stealthy cat. I drew in a shaky breath. They must have instructed her to bring me here. And to leave me alone.

I scanned the perimeter of the trees. My goddess eyesight was gone and I could see nothing lurking near me. But I knew they must be close. There was no point to any of this if they were not. The sun had dipped even lower in the sky and it was dangling now on the edge of the horizon. With its departure, the blackness of night drew rapidly upon us.

I studied the clearing once again. It was a perfect circle, full of knee high wild grass and encircled by tropical trees.

"A perfect circle," I mused again to myself. "It must be symbolic of something. But what?"

"You're such a smart, smart girl," a voice creaked.

Stepping from the edge of the tree line, Lachesis walked steadily toward me, in her ancient, stooped form. Not only was she ancient, but I was also quite aware that she had been rendered powerless, so I stood unafraid and waiting as she approached.

"You're such a proud little thing," she observed. I stuck my chin out even further and she smiled. "You always have been. That's a paradox. Pride really should go against your peaceful nature."

"I am meant to bring contentment and peace to those around me," I replied. "It does not mean that I always feel it myself. Of course I do not- particularly when there are those who continually endanger the peace that I love."

She smiled again.

"Subtly is not a strength that you possess," she observed. "I like that."

"I care not what you like," I answered. "Please tell me where my mother is. You have no need for her. I'm the one you want."

"And to get you here, we had to involve your mother. She is restrained and you are outnumbered."

I felt many sets of eyes on me and my gaze flew once again to the tree line. I could see shadows of quite a few people surrounding us. Calypso's nymphs. They were under the orders of the Fates. I swallowed.

"I am outnumbered now, but you are familiar with my father... the god of war. He will be along shortly."

She laughed, a haunting sound.

"I wouldn't count on that, I'm afraid. It is possible that they might have been... shall we say... waylaid." She laughed again, satisfied and secure. "I fear they will be of no help to you."

"Yes, you sound very afraid," I muttered.

"Come now," she extended her hand. "There is a party and we're waiting for you."

I ignored her hand. Did she really believe that I was going to actually touch her? I followed closely behind her as she moved with surprising speed through the clearing. As we crossed through the trees, the solemn nymphs parted and allowed us to pass. Their expressions were at once curious, sorrowful and resigned. I could sense that they didn't wish to be participants, but they had no choice.

A few minutes later, we stood in what had to be the very center of Ogygia. On one end of the encampment, a magnificently large black tent stood proudly, its fabric rippling with the gentle breeze. Facing it from the other end of the encampment was another tent, this one as red as blood.

In the middle, was an enormous pit. It spit fire, the flames licking the edges of the pit itself as it roared within. A fire pit. Perfect.

But that wasn't the worst part. Hanging upside down like bats from the trees above us were so many minor gods and goddesses that I could not count them all. From where I stood, I could see Alathea, Eris, Eros and Chaos. There had to be at least 30 more, but I couldn't see their faces from here.

They were suspended in the air, held by long golden cords fastened at their ankles. Their hands were criss-crossed over their chests and held tight by an odd looking sheer material that surrounded their entire bodies. Only their hair was free and dangled downward toward the flame. Their eyes were tightly closed. It was as if they were in a strange, comatose state, much like how we found the Amazons in Eris' home.

"Eris helped you," I pointed out. "She delivered Aphrodite to you. Why would you turn on her?"

"Why do you care?" Lachesis asked. "She is your sworn enemy."

"True," I acknowledged. "And I don't care. I was simply curious."

"Well, you know what curiosity did to the cat." Lachesis smiled a slow, creepy smile at me.

"What do you hope to gain here?" I asked her. "What have these people done to you?"

"Absolutely nothing," she replied with a smug smile. "But they will be used as a message."

"Of what?" I asked in frustration.

"Of things that aren't your concern." Another voice resounded through the encampment and I looked up to see Atropos and Clothos emerging from the black tent. They slowly walked to the edge of the fire where I stood with Lachesis.

"You do not have the right to demand knowledge from us," Clothos snapped in her superior way.

"Yet you cannot stop me, can you?" I asked. "You possess no magic here." I looked to Atropos. "Your breaths are no longer hazardous to me." Her ancient eyes snapped and I could see how much being rendered powerless truly vexed her.

From the opposite end, three hooded figured emerged from the red tent. The Keres. I watched them with interest as they crept to where we stood. When they reached us, I gazed at them curiously. And gasped.

They were hideous. It was no wonder they wore hoods. Their faces were ancient, like the Fates, but their skin looked like cracked stone. Their cloudy eyes were almost white and blood ran from the corners and dripped from their eyelashes to the ground. Everywhere they walked, they trailed blood.

"Do we repulse you?" the one nearest to me asked. I decided not to lie.

"Yes."

She smiled and grew even more terrifying as her gaunt face stretched over her jagged bones.

"We weep blood because of all that we have seen," she uttered. Reaching out a gnarled finger, she trailed it along my jawbone. "Such beauty," she hissed.

"If you had seen even a portion of what we have, you would not be so pure," she finished, dropping her hand back to her side. "Our sisters have damned us to a lifetime of suffering due to the evil that we have witnessed."

"Much of it at your own hands," Clothos reminded her. "You are not innocent, sister."

The Keres shook their heads. "As if we had a choice," the one in the middle croaked.

Lachesis stepped in. "That is neither here nor there. We have other things to attend to. It is time that we filled dear Harmonia in our plans."

"So, tell me."

I tried to sound brave and sincerely hoped that I carried it off. They could not read my mind here, something that worked in my favor. They were out of their element.

"We have brought you here to give you a choice," Clothos stated.

I waited through the long pause as they all watched me.

"And that is?" I prompted, when their silence continued.

The Fates' grinned, all of them in unison. It was a startlingly frightening sight. I steeled myself for whatever atrocity that they would reveal. I didn't have to wait long.

"Your life for theirs."

Lachesis motioned toward all of the gods dangling lifelessly over the fire.

"Your mother is there," she confirmed as she watched my gaze flit over each face. "And there is just one more thing...."

Cadmus stepped from the shadows, his face blank and silent.

"Step forward," Lachesis commanded him.

He silently moved forward until he stood in front of her, directly beside me.

"Cadmus!" I cried, grabbing his strong arm.

He didn't even blink. It was if I had said nothing at all.

"Cadmus!" I cried again as I shook his arm. His eyes stared impassively past me as if he were in a trance.

"What have you done to him?" I demanded, whirling to face the Fates. "Magic doesn't work here. How have you done this?"

"Ah, sweet Harmonia," Clothos mocked me. "You simply don't think things through. Of course magic cannot be rendered here. But magical spells that are timed correctly can be effective."

I stared at her in confusion, trying to make sense of her words.

"It's a well-timed spell," she declared simply. "It was administered by Eris at the same time as her love potion. It was meant to become active as he crossed the sea and landed on these shores. He became our agent, leading your father and the Amazons straight to us. They are up there also." She gestured proudly to the trees above us. "Calypso's nymphs are quite nimble and strong. This is all their handiwork."

I struggled with the simple act of breathing, an exercise in futility as soon as she spoke her next words.

"Cadmus," she ordered. "Step forward."

He obediently walked directly toward the fire.

Chapter Seventeen

I screamed and grabbed Cadmus, pulling with all of my might on his arms, trying to force him to stop moving. It was no use. He was much too strong and shook me off as easily as if I were a feather.

"Stop!" I screamed to Lachesis. "Please, I'll do anything."

"Anything?" she asked, with her eyebrow raised.

"Yes. Anything," I promised.

"Cadmus, stop," she ordered. He halted with one foot hovering over the fire.

"Step back."

He took one step backward, standing as still as a statue, staring blankly straight ahead and I breathed a small sigh of relief. But my relief was short lived. Lachesis turned to me with an arrogant, knowing expression on her weathered face.

"Your life for theirs?" she asked politely.

I nodded. "My life for theirs."

"This was easier than we thought, sisters," she murmured in amusement.

They shared satisfied grins and I felt nausea rising in my belly.

"Too easy, though," she mused. "It's not nearly satisfying enough. Alexi?" she called.

Alexi stepped from the opposite side of the pit with his expressionless face. He was firmly grasping the elbow of my mother. My mortal mother.

Shoving her forward, she stopped limply next to the edge of the fire. The flames leaped from the massive hole and licked at their feet. I could smell the singed hair of the gods and goddesses hanging upside down above it and I flinched. My mother's face was as stone, as emotionless as Cadmus'. She was enchanted, too.

"We can't let you have both of them," Clothos said smoothly. "That would be so unlike us. What would people think? You may choose one. And then of course, you can have the rest of them." She motioned above our heads, as though the gods hanging over us were worthless chattel.

"I must choose Cadmus or my mortal mother?" I asked incredulously. "Lachesis, that's unnecessary. I'm giving you my life willingly. I'm handing it to you. It's yours. Take it."

Lachesis laughed. "And we thank you. But we must have our amusement, too. Which one will you choose?"

I stared at my mother's helpless form. She was so vulnerable and delicately human. I wondered if Alexi had taken her against her will or bewitched her to get her here. Or maybe he had even lied and told her that I needed her, in which case she would have come willingly which made it all the worse. Her dark hair, just like mine, glistened in the light from the fire.

My gaze shifted to my soul mate. He stood silently next to me, his muscles taut and poised for movement, but rendered useless by the strange spell. All the strength in the world was useless if your mind was captive. His liquid dark eyes stared straight ahead, completely oblivious to my agony.

"No." I murmured. "I cannot."

"I thought you might say that," Lachesis grinned. "Which means that you all shall die."

A thought came to me, something I had forgotten. "You cannot kill them. It takes Zeus' sword to kill an immortal. And you don't have it."

Annoyance flashed upon her face.

"Correct. But we will find it. In the meantime, your precious friends and family will burn in this fire in torment until we find the sword and put them out of their misery. Your mortal mother, of course, can so easily die. Perhaps it would be more humane to choose her, Keeper. Her death will be quick. If you choose Cadmus, you can suffer together."

"You would burn us alive until you find the sword?" I repeated in horror.

"Now you're catching on," Lachesis nodded. "There is one small thing though. One little thing. There is a box, a box containing murderous souls. We know that Ahmose took it for you. If you tell us where it is, we'll let both Cadmus and your mother live. Only you need to die. What do you think about this bargain?"

"I can't give it to you," I murmured uncertainly.

But even as I spoke, my eyes turned once again to Cadmus and my mother. I thought of Ares and Aphrodite... their laughing faces from happier times. I thought of Cadmus' chocolate eyes sparkling into mine as he grinned. And I knew, in the space of that one second, that I would gladly do it. I would give them exactly what they wanted and I would exchange my life for theirs. I would gladly burn in the pit for eternity to save them.

Thanks to the Fates, I had a couple thousand years of practice at dealing with sadness and tragedy. I could do this. I could put aside fear and sadness and do what I needed to do.

"You have prepared me well for this day," I said to them calmly. "But tell me, how do I know that you will stand by your side of the bargain? How do I know that you will release everyone else?"

"Harmonia, use your head," Clothos answered. "You will be alive in this pit until we find the sword. You will see us release everyone. You will be in agony, but you will be conscious. That is part of the fun."

I thought on that for a moment.

"Alright. We have a deal. I will give you the box on one condition. Let me say goodbye to them. Please. Restore their consciousness so that I can tell them goodbye. I have never knowingly done anything to offend you or against you. I have done all that you have asked for thousands of years. Please. Can't you do this one thing for me?"

I hated pleading with them. I hated it more than anything I had ever done. My hatred for them completely filled me up. But if I could just look into Cadmus' eyes one more time and see the love that he held for me there... it would be worth it. I could willingly step to my death.

"Give us a moment," Lachesis demanded.

She and the other two Fates convened in a huddle. I stood quietly, my gaze flitting from each suspended god and goddess to my mother and Cadmus. A moment later, the old hags turned.

"Fine," Lachesis answered simply. "Where is the box?"

I slid my knapsack off of my back and pulled out the box. I handed it to her with shaking fingers. One of the ancient Keres started to say something, but at Lachesis' glare, she closed her mouth and remained silent.

Lachesis motioned to a group of nymphs hovering nearby in the trees and then gestured toward Cadmus and my mother.

"Restrain them."

The nymphs stepped forward reluctantly and did as she asked.

"I would also like to say goodbye to Ares and Aphrodite," I demanded.

Lachesis narrowed her eyes at me, but still gestured toward another nymph.

"Get them down," she instructed. She turned back to me. "No tricks."

I shook my head. "No. No tricks."

I watched a couple of smaller nymphs shimmy spritely up the trees to the cocoons that my mother and father were restrained in. Pushing them, they swung the strange looking pods toward other servants waiting to catch them. Yet another servant released a pulley which lowered my parents safely to the ground.

Within a few minutes, they were unwrapped and stood lifelessly next to Cadmus and my mother. My mother's silvery eyes shone in the firelight, but they were as empty as everyone else's. I sighed heavily. It was heartbreaking and I was helpless.

Lachesis turned to them and walked from person to person, stopping to murmur something in each one's ear. And one by one, the life returned to their eyes. As soon as they looked around and realized where they were, they began struggling hard against the nymphs' restraining holds.

But it was no use.

"What is the meaning of this?" Ares roared. Cadmus sought my gaze and I watched as realization dawned on his handsome face.

"Why are you here?" he asked me. "What is this?"

"I'm here because I'm the only one who can save you," I murmured as I stepped to him. "I love you so much." I traced his face with my hand, lingering over his lips. His dark eyes were panicked.

"Harmonia, I don't know what you are thinking, but whatever it is, put it out of your mind."

He desperately tried to hold my gaze, but I moved forward to Aphrodite and Ares. In their faces, I found such familiarity and comfort. Aphrodite was outraged, her lovely face practically shooting sparks.

"You will wish you had never even existed," she spit toward the Fates. "Release us this instant."

"Mother," I murmured. "You will be released soon. Please, protect Cadmus and see that my mother gets safely back home."

Aphrodite stared at me anxiously. "Of course, I will. But where do you plan on being? You are always with me, right at my side. That should not change. I won't have it!"

"For once, mother, you aren't going to have a choice."

I kissed her lightly on the cheek and moved to Ares. He stood before me with a gaze like thunder. I vaguely remembered the time he had rescued me from Cleopatra's golden barge. He had been wearing much the same expression at the time. I smiled at him, cupping his face.

"I love you, father. Avenge this."

He nodded. "I will avenge everything." I did not doubt him. Fury simmered in his eyes, turning them almost black. He was the only one of the Olympic gods who didn't possess the strange silver eye color. I hugged him quickly and moved again.

I stood in front of my mortal mother. She stared around us in bewilderment, unable to comprehend where we were or what was going on. I couldn't blame her. It was so far beyond her reality that it was crazy. And as a mortal, she was immersed in the haze of this island much more quickly.

"Mom, I want you to know that I love you, okay?"

She nodded quietly. "And I love you. But what we are doing here? Am I dreaming?"

I nodded, watching her eyes fill up with the bewilderment that this island induced.

"Yes, you're dreaming. Go back to sleep now. I'll see you in the morning."

With wide eyes, she murmured an agreement. I choked back my tears as I motioned to Lachesis and my mother's face once again went slack and lifeless. She did not need to see what was coming. Her mortal mind would break from it.

Out of the corner of my eye, I saw Ares and Cadmus still struggling against the restraining hold of the nymphs. I moved once again to Cadmus and kissed him softly.

"Cadmus, I love you. Forever. Remember that." I felt a tear escape the corner of my eye and slide hotly down my cheek.

"Harmonia, don't," he pleaded, his eyes full of pain. "Please, I'm begging you."

I pressed one more kiss to his lips and then turned away from him while I still could.

"Okay," I mumbled, taking a deep breath. "I'm ready."

I ignored the frantic protests from my family and Cadmus as I stood numbly in front of the Moirae. I felt my bloodstone lying limp and silently against my chest like the cold lump of stone that it was. It couldn't help me here. Nothing could.

As I stood waiting for what seemed like an eternity, every feeling that I'd ever had, both goddess and mortal, flooded back to me with a vengeance. My lives flashed before my eyes- good memories and bad ones- and in that moment, none of the sadness mattered. Because no matter what life I led, no matter what sadness it contained, it was always outweighed by the joy and happiness that I found with my soul mate and my family. I had been very blessed.

As I bowed my head, I felt a strange fog descend upon me and I realized with a start that it was the effects of Ogygia. It was beginning to steal my consciousness. Very soon, I would forget my purpose here.

"Do it!" I hissed.

"Do what?" Lachesis asked me in amusement. "It is for you to do, Keeper."

I eyed the ledge of the pit. It was so close. Just two steps away. I took a shaking step.

Then one more.

I stood with my toes curled around the edge, ignoring the shouts and protests of the others as I felt the warmth of the fire heat my legs and my face. The orange flames were mesmerizing and I stared into them. Soon, I would be among them. And I wanted to do it while I was focused on the love that I felt while I could still remember it. Conjuring every peaceful feeling that I could, I drew upon my inner strength. Picturing Cadmus' beautiful face, I lifted my foot.

"Wait!" a voice hissed. Keeping my foot poised in mid-air, I turned my head slightly.

A Keres had broken rank and moved forward.

"Wait!" she repeated.

"What are you doing?" Clothos demanded of her. But the old Keres ignored her, keeping her cloudy eyes fixed upon mine.

"Harmonia, remember," she instructed. "Remember! It is made from feathers and flame."

At the old hag's words, as if someone had flipped a switch, a memory did form in my mind. A magnificent crimson bird with iridescent feathers and azure eyes. A bird that built a funeral pyre for itself and then lit it on fire...dying in its own flame. I could see it as clearly in my mind as if it stood in front of me. I glanced at my wrist. I had the mark and it was pulsing erratically right this moment.

I was the Phoenix, the Chosen One.

"Yesssss," she hissed. "You remember."

I nodded and turned my head toward Cadmus. "I love you."

And I stepped from the ledge.

The heat swallowed me up, consuming my breath as I fell, but it didn't burn me. Oranges and reds swirled together as the flames rushed past. Time seemed to stand still as I moved in slow motion and I was suddenly no longer plunging toward agony. A gush of cool air swirled around me and lifted me from the pit, throwing me up and backward. I landed in a sprawled heap on the ground, safely out of harm's way.

Looking up in amazement, I saw a Phoenix, magnificent and beautiful, rising from the ground. Every flame contained in the pit was now swirling into the massive bird as it flew upward with wings of fire. Its eyes were a brilliant and vivid blue and they were trained on me as it shrieked a deafening roar.

I clapped my hands over my ears as it flew into the sky, circling above us as it lit up the night with its glory. I was astounded. This island didn't permit magic. Yet the Phoenix appeared to be unconstrained by anything at all.

And it had taken every lick of the fire with it. The pit was empty now and harmless. The Fates could no longer use innocent lives as leverage. Their threats were empty. The nymphs realized it at the same moment that I did. They released my parents and Cadmus, while several others leaped into the trees to lower the captive gods.

Cadmus rushed to me, scooping me into his strong arms. His gentle kiss was the last thing I felt before the fog of the island overtook me.

Chapter Eighteen

$\mathscr{I}$opened my eyes and found Cadmus staring into mine.

I startled and leaned up on my elbows, looking frantically around me. But there was no reason to panic. I was in bed, safe and sound.

I was in Zeus' palace and daylight was streaming through the open balcony doors. Sheer curtains fluttered in the wind, bringing with it the pungently floral scent of the Olympic breeze. I inhaled deeply, tasting the flowers on my tongue, as I tried to gain my bearings. I turned to Cadmus.

"How did we get here?"

He drew me into his arms, pulling me close, and I melted into his embrace. How could I help it? There was nowhere else I would rather be, no matter how we managed to get here. I inhaled his masculine scent, clinging to his strength like a drowning person to a life raft.

After a few moments, he ended the kiss, although he didn't loosen his hold on me.

"If you ever do that to me again," he began with a stern look on his face, "I will beat you. Don't look at me like that. I will hang you in the dungeons of this palace myself and I will beat you within an inch of your life."

I stared at him dubiously, still stroking his arm.

"Don't doubt it," he added. "You almost gave me a heart attack. If you would've…if you…"

His jaw clenched as his voice trailed off and I stroked his face with trembling fingers.

"I know," I murmured softly. "I love you, too."

He nodded.

"Where is everyone?" I asked. "How did we get here?"

"Hecate," he answered. "Remember, she said we would need her three times. The third time was rescuing us from the island. She apparently sensed when the time was right and willed us back here."

"And my mother? My mortal mother?" I clarified.

He hesitated. "She's on the island with Calypso."

"What?" I jerked my head up. "Why would Hecate leave her there? We've got to go back and…"

Cadmus smoothly interrupted. "She left her there because she wasn't sure what to do with her. It's not safe for a mortal to linger in the Spiritlands for long and Hecate couldn't send her to Pasadena, because your mother would wonder at your absence. Calypso's island is safe for her. We are going to be busy for awhile. We have a sword to find."

I had forgotten about the sword in all of the excitement of almost burning alive. I nodded slowly in understanding.

I pictured my mother wandering through the paradise of Ogygia, and I sighed. There were worse places to keep her. I'd have to think more on this one.

"And Aphrodite?" I asked anxiously.

I'd barely gotten the words out of my mouth though, when Aphrodite herself barged into the bedchambers. She looked beautiful, as fresh as if she'd just come from a spa day. Her silvery eyes though, were crackling like lightning.

"Harmonia!" she snapped as she dropped onto the bed at my side. "If you ever, and by ever, I mean at any time throughout the rest of eternity, decide to do something so foolish again, I will personally …"

I cut her off by grabbing her in a big hug. She stopped talking as she hugged me back and I felt the wetness of her tears against my neck. As she pulled away, she wiped at them.

"I love you, too," I told her quietly. She smiled.

"I know." She paused to look at me. "Your father is very agitated with you, you know."

"Really?" I studied her doubtfully. It seemed more in his nature to be proud of my cunning and courage. And I could see on her face that I was right, but I didn't point it out. I simply let her nod.

"Yes, Harmonia. He is fit to be tied. You should probably give him a while to calm down before you talk to him."

Hmm. That meant I should probably give him awhile so that his proud accolades didn't completely trash her story. In my good mood though, I felt generous. I'd go along with it.

"Alright. I'll give him an hour or so before I seek him out," I agreed. She nodded, satisfied that her fibs were safe. I had to shake my head. In every life, she had been exactly the same. Colorful and excitable.

She rose from the bed, raising one perfectly sculpted eyebrow at Cadmus and me.

"I was just going to sit on the veranda and have breakfast. Would you like to join me or will you, er, be awhile?"

I felt my cheeks explode into flame.

"No, we'll be happy to join you," I replied quickly. "Just give us a few minutes." At her grin, I quickly corrected myself. "A minute. *One*."

She laughed, a sound that echoed through the room like a peal of clear bells and I smiled. Just a little while ago, I thought my life was over. And now, here I was, joking and smiling with those that I loved. Life was truly amazing.

"I'll see you outside," she grinned. "Don't take too long."

And she was gone, ducking out the door and leaving us alone. I turned to Cadmus.

"You have one minute," I told him with a smile as I ducked back under the covers.

"Challenge accepted," he chuckled as he followed me, throwing the coverlet back over our heads.

My soul mate does so love a challenge.

* * *

When we met Aphrodite on the veranda a short while later, she was seated facing the city, across from the Keres. I studied them as we crossed the courtyard. They were still just as frightening as they were on Ogygia. Haggard, stooped and ancient. We did not make a sound as we walked, yet they turned in perfect unison to face us with nearly sightless eyes.

"Harmonia," the one nearest to me creaked. "We've not been properly introduced." She held out her gnarled, wrinkled hand. "I am Moros."

I knelt at her feet, grasping her hand. "I'm pleased to meet you."

"Thank you for acting with such bravery," she said with a nod. "We were right about you all along. I knew that you would act with honor. There were those," she rolled her eyes at her sisters, "that doubted. But I did not."

I hesitated. "I don't understand, Moros. Were you never with the Moirae? What part did Annen play? And where is he?"

"No. We were never with the Moirae, we simply tricked them into believing that we were. They should not hold the throne and they have been wrong for a long time. But we had to bide our time and wait for the prophecy to come to pass. Annen is safe and sound. He is running an errand for us right now. There are so many things to do now, as I'm sure you can imagine."

"His tongue...you didn't..." I looked nervously at the sisters.

"No, child. That was the Moirae. They tried to test his loyalty and torture him into revealing our secrets. He did not fold, much like his brother Ahmose."

My head snapped up. "They were brothers?"

She nodded her ancient head in unison with her two sisters. "Yes. And he is very disturbed over his brother's death."

I could understand that.

"Where are the Fates?" I asked my mother. "What shall be done with them?"

"They are being held on Ogygia in the empty pit that was filled with fire. No one is mistreating them. We will hold them there until Zeus is restored and he can deal with them as he would like."

"And Alexi?"

"He is there with them, as well as Eris." I felt a stab of intense satisfaction at that. That girl deserved the pit more than anyone.

"Where is the box of souls?" I shivered. The mere thought unnerved me. My mother patted my arm soothingly.

"We are keeping it safe until Zeus is restored. He can handle it as he wishes."

"It seems that the loose ends have been tied up," I observed. "How long was I sleeping?"

"Only overnight, sweetling," she replied. "You deserved the rest. You looked quite peaked when we returned."

"Yes," I mumbled. "Facing a fiery death will do that to a person." She rolled her silver eyes.

"Harmonia, you're always so dramatic."

She smiled and I knew that she was relieved and happy to be back to our normal sarcastic banter. We were so comfortable together.

Still stroking my arm, she continued.

"I was thinking that we would host a dinner tonight. We'll invite everyone that we brought back from the island and as well as the witches. The near future will be challenging as we seek the sword and find the other Olympic gods. One lavish party would do wonders for everyone's spirit. What say you?"

"I say that you will use any excuse to throw a party. But it's a good idea. The mood around Olympus is so somber. It needs lightened. Where is everyone else, by the way?" I glanced around us and the palace did seem empty, except for us.

"Why, they have returned to their homes, of course, to rebuild. Most of them have been held on Calypso's Island for so long that their homes have fallen to rubble. Ares has gone out to survey the damages. And Ortrera and her Amazons have taken the little girl back to the island for us. They will return later. Your father has commanded it, even though they would much prefer to return to their home."

She looked dismayed at their unhappiness and to be honest, I agreed. If they wanted to return to their home in the wilds of the Spiritlands, they should be allowed to do so. They'd been instrumental in the rescue. I made a mental note to discuss it with Ares.

I straightened from my crouch and nodded to the Keres.

"It was very nice to formerly meet you. I cannot thank you enough for forcing me to remember that I can command the Phoenix. Without that, all would have been lost."

"The pleasure was ours," Moros said with a ghastly smile. I tried not to shudder as I returned it.

I turned to Cadmus.

"I'd like to walk through the city, if you don't mind."

He held out his arm. "Your wish is my command, my lady," he bowed. Aphrodite smiled gently as she watched us.

"I will see you this evening," I told her. "Stay out of trouble until then."

I took Cadmus' arm and we strolled from the courtyard.

Passing through a cavernous room of the palace, we came across Hephaestus as he lugged large pieces of rubble through the white stone rooms, piling them outdoors. It appeared that he was already at work to create new luxurious furnishings. He could have lifted one hand and restored it all in a blink, but he had always liked physical labor. He nodded at us as we walked past. Other servants called in from around the Spiritlands were milling around like worker bees as they put the palace back in order. I felt a sense of satisfaction that everything was falling back into place.

As we strolled over the gray cobble-stone walks, I turned to Cadmus.

"What should we do about my mother? I can't just leave her on the island, but I can't send her home without me, either. It's a quandary."

I stared absently past him as I watched Alathea putting her pillaged home to rights across the bustling street. She nodded her head toward the crumbling marble pillars and they rebuilt themselves in front of my eyes, tall and strong. As she turned to wave at me, the window behind her continued to wash itself.

"Harmonia! So glad to see you are well," she called. "You fulfilled your promise and came for me. I thank you." She dipped her head and I smiled.

"You're welcome, of course. Thank you for risking so much to bring me the Map of Souls," I replied. "Hecate has it safely tucked into her libraries."

"I know," she answered. "I spoke with her this morning." She smiled again and hummed as she went about her work. I was so happy to see her so safe and sound. The last two times I had seen her had not been so pleasant.

"Going back to your question," Cadmus said, "I don't see the problem with leaving her safely on Ogygia. She will be out of harm's way and will be none the wiser regarding what is going on. She'll be in paradise and she'll keep Calypso company. She'll enjoy her time there and then we'll retrieve her."

"And then?" I asked. "What then?"

"You mean, what should we do at that time—should we remain here?" He raised an eyebrow. "We can make that decision when we come to it. We've got a few bridges to cross before then."

"I know that's right," I muttered. But as we walked, the day was so beautiful that I just wanted to put it all out of my mind. We had stared death in the face and come back from it. We definitely deserved a day off.

So, we spent the day enjoying each other's company. We laughed and picked fresh lotus blossoms and fed them to each other next to the stream. We laid in the velvety grass and talked for a couple of hours about nothing and then finally, I fell asleep on his hard chest and we napped in the shade. My last conscious thought was how comfortable I was with his strong arms wrapped around me.

It was nightfall before he finally woke me up.

I raised my head and stared at the twinkling stars and the swirling dark sky of the Spiritlands. "Maybe we should just stay here and not go to Aphrodite's dinner," I suggested.

"Hmm. I see a couple of problems with that," Cadmus replied with a grin. "First, Aphrodite will kill us both. Second, the Chimeras will be out soon. And honestly, I don't know who I would rather face. An angry Aphrodite or a hungry Chimera."

"I'd take the Chimera any day," I laughed as I sat up and pulled him to his feet. He flattened me to his chest as he stood and kissed me long and sound.

"It feels good to be here with you," he admitted. "I think we should consider staying."

I nodded solemnly. "I know. I was thinking the same thing. We belong here. But as you said, we can cross that bridge later."

We made our way quickly back to the palace and I stood in utter shock when we reached it. It had been almost completely transformed to its former glory. Light poured from its every window, door and balcony, making it a truly beautiful beacon in the night. It looked every bit as magical as I knew that it was.

When we reached the grand staircase, we parted ways. I kissed Cadmus quickly and promised to be back down stairs within a few minutes, then kissed him one more lingering time.

"I just need to freshen up," I said breathlessly as he pulled away the second time. "I'll be right back."

"I'll be waiting," he promised, his beautiful dark eyes gleaming.

Bounding up the stairs, I hurried for my room to change clothes and straighten my hair. I quickly changed into a long white sheath wrapped with a thick golden belt and then stared into the mirror to pile my dark hair onto my head. I felt a little plain, so I conjured up a matching set of jade combs and they appeared in my hand. I tucked them into my hair and examined myself. I would do.

Turning to rush back out the door, I stopped in place.

My balcony doors were open and one of the Keres stood facing me as she leaned against the railing. Blood from her eyes was pooling around her feet, so she had clearly been waiting for me for awhile. Her dark cloak fluttered as the wind blew around her. At the expression on her face, my heart immediately froze.

"What are you doing here?" I asked, trying to remain calm.

"Come here, Harmonia," she instructed.

Obligingly, I walked numbly to where she stood as she turned and faced the courtyard.

"Look below us, Harmonia. Isn't it beautiful?"

I gazed below us and it truly was beautiful. Lanterns hung from every surrounding tree, creating a soft, delicate glow. Guests mingled and laughed as they drank nectar and enjoyed our newly found carefree feeling. A pall felt as though it had been lifted and I could see the lightness of being reflected on every face in attendance. Even Ortrera and her warriors seemed a bit more relaxed than usual as they lingered on the edge of the festivities. Aphrodite and Ares, of course, were in the middle of everything, laughing and dancing to music that no one else could hear.

"Look at Cadmus," the old hag breathed into my ear. "Your husband is a handsome man, Harmonia. You are quite fortunate."

Cadmus stood next to Ortrera as he calmly watched everyone celebrating around him. The angles of his bronzed face caught the flickers of candlelight perfectly and his beauty did take my breath away. He was patient as he waited for me, confident that I would arrive at his side at any moment.

And each moment, I doubted that fact more and more.

I turned to Moros. "Why are you here?"

"Because the sword must be found, Harmonia."

I shook my head in annoyance. "I realize that. We will begin the search tomorrow. We'll find it."

"But how committed are you? To what lengths will you go?"

"Great lengths. Olympus must be restored. I understand the importance."

Moros studied me for a long moment. "I believe you. But not for the reason that you think. You know, you were never told the rest of the prophecy."

I felt my heart thudding against my chest as I returned her stare as calmly as I could.

"There is more? What is the rest?"

"It has been said that the Chosen One will fight for the crown only after a great loss."

"A great loss?" I repeated in confusion. "What do you mean?"

"We think that you need to lose someone you love in order to spur you to action."

I shook my head slowly from side to side as I grasped what she was saying. What she was threatening.

"No. Moros, that's not necessary. I will find the sword. I am fully committed. I need to lose no one. I have only just gotten everyone back."

"You know the power of the sword, Harmonia. Not only is it the only existing thing that can kill an immortal, but the holder of the sword has the ability to also *restore* life." She grinned a twisted smile. "Perhaps you need incentive to find it quickly. Look at your lover again, Harmonia."

Breathlessly, I did as she requested.

Cadmus was now standing with Moros' sister. He was talking with her in earnest, although he did not seem bothered or upset. That much was a relief. Annen stood at his elbow, his dark eyes locked with mine. I struggled to breathe.

"My sister... you never formally met her," Moros pointed out.

"You're right, I did not," I agreed. "I shall have to make a point of doing so."

"You shall," Moros agreed. "Her name is Thanatos."

"Thanatos," I whispered and her name froze on my lips as a chill spread from my head to my toes.

It meant death.

My gaze flew back to Cadmus. He was gone. My scream split the night and then I saw nothing.

THE END

Read more about Cadmus and Harmonia in Book Three of
The Bloodstone Saga
Coming in Fall 2011

About the Author

Courtney Cole is a YA novelist who loves Lake Michigan but is terrified of buoys and sea gulls. That makes for some interesting days at the beach. She was born and raised in Kansas where it is too hot in the summer to do anything but read. So growing up, she read stacks and stacks of books. She learned from an early age that if she didn't like an ending, she could just write her own. And that's how she knew that she had a writer's heart.

She migrated from Kansas to northern Indiana, just a stone's throw from Chicago and Lake Michigan. She lives in the suburbs with her real life Prince Charming, her ornery kids (there is a small chance that they get their orneriness from their mother) and small domestic zoo.

To learn more about Courtney and her books, visit her website at:

www.courtneycolewrites.com

Other books by Courtney Cole:
Every Last Kiss (Book One of the Bloodstone Saga)
Princess
Guardian

All titles are available on Amazon and Barnes and Noble.com

Author's Notes

$\mathscr{I}$ occurred to me that you might be wondering why I started this series out the way that I did. I could have easily began everything in Olympus, but I didn't think that would truly get Harmonia's past across. I really wanted to illustrate how the Fates have tormented poor Harmonia throughout the millennia. In *Every Last Kiss*, I tried to provide an up close picture of the kind of tragic life that the Fates have inflicted on Harmonia time and time again.

So many people have remarked, "Wow, you must really love Egyptian culture or the Cleopatra era," after they read *Every Last Kiss*. I suppose that is true. I have always found that period of time (and Cleopatra herself) fascinating, which is one of the reasons why I chose it to begin Harmonia's story in this series.

But I've also always been fascinated by Greek mythology. The magical element of it lures me in and that is how I ended up with this storyline. Anything can happen when you are dealing with magical worlds and that is something that appeals to me. I can truly flex my creative muscle when dabbling in it.

Quite a lot in this book is based on real myth. Harmonia and Cadmus are actual mythological figures, as well as all of the other gods and goddesses that I wrote of here. I twisted their abilities and gifts to suit my purposes in some instances, but for the most part, I did try to stay true to what is already written about them.

Except for Ares. It is written that Ares is bloodthirsty and heinous. But that isn't what I wanted him to be, so I pretty much changed him entirely. I wanted my god of war to be ferocious and fierce when need be, but funny, kind and loving also. I like him ever so much better my way.

Harmonia's Necklace is a real legend which played into my story perfectly. Of course, I did alter it a bit to fit my storyline, just as I did some of the other mythological elements.

The Spiritlands is entirely a figment of my imagination. I began wondering... you hear of Mount Olympus, where the twelve Olympic gods and goddesses live, but where in the world do the minor gods and goddesses live? And that is how the Spiritlands came to be.

My point here is... if you are someone who studies Greek Mythology, please take no offense if I altered something for my purposes. This is a work of fiction and my imagination is a very contrary thing- I can barely control it.

And finally, about the ending. What can I say? I love a good cliffhanger.

Acknowledgements

*O*ne thing I have discovered is that it takes the support of *many* people for an author to successfully write a book.

As always, I need to thank my family first and foremost. Thank you so much for putting up with me when I write and plot and daydream about my characters. Your support keeps me going and you'll never know how much I appreciate it.

To my girls, Wren Emerson and M. Leighton. You ladies are two amazing goddesses yourselves. Without your writer-ly support, I doubt I would be able to function. Thank you for everything.

Dani Snell... Thank you so much for being a truly awesome beta reader. Your input is incredible and valuable and I really, really appreciate it. I feel like I discovered gold when I found you!

Tammy Luke- my talented cover artist/magician. Thank you a million times over for being so patient and professional as you work with me and create your magic. You truly bring my visions to life.

And finally, I'd like to thank the readers who read my work. Thank you for reading it, thanking you for reviewing it and thank you so much for the emails telling me how much you love it. It is music to a writer's ears. I can't tell you how many times you have truly made my day. Thank you.

www.ingramcontent.com/pod-product-compliance
Lightning Source LLC
Chambersburg PA
CBHW050928120626
46552CB00001B/88